MARKETS ANTHOLOGY FOR THE OLGA SINCLAIR OPEN SHORT STORY COMPETITION

2018

Compiled and edited by Kathy Joy

Cover image created by Maureen Nisbet.

Acknowledgements

The Norwich Writers' Circle would like to thank our adjudicators, crime novelist Alison Bruce and author Lynsey White for reading and judging the entries and for completing the difficult task of choosing the winners.

We'd also like to thank Norwich City Council and particularly to Kristina Fox, Norwich Market manager for allowing us to promote the competition throughout the market place.

Finally, we would finally like to express our gratitude to everyone who entered the competition and to the winning authors for allowing us to showcase their stories in this anthology.

CONTENTS

A TRIBUTE TO OLGA SINCLAIR

By Anne Funnell

Olga Sinclair passed away on April 28th, 2014, aged 91.

She left us a surprise legacy in her will. This donation to our funds has supported our annual Open Prose Competition ever since. For the benefit of those reading this anthology who may not know anything about her, I have been asked to write an introduction.

Olga joined the Norwich Writers' Circle in 1960, aged 37. Within seven years, she had published her first book for children with Blackwell's, followed by 4 others. She published 25 books altogether under the names of Ellen Clare, Olga Daniels, and her married name of Olga Sinclair, with several other publishers, depending on the genre. She wrote romantic historical fiction sticking as far as possible to the facts, which she meticulously researched. I remember her telling me of a visit to Scotland, and the book she wrote afterwards called, Gretna Green (A romantic History). The last book she wrote was called The Countess and the Miner, published in 2005 by Robert Hale.

For Poppyland she wrote two historical books, When Wherries Sailed By (1987) and Potter Heigham (The Heart of Broadland) (1989).

She acted as Magistrate for several years, giving her an understanding of current affairs and local issues.

In 1968 she became a committee member for the Circle, and she was the Hon Treasurer for a couple of years. She became Vice-President in 1980. After Mary Ingate died in 1991, she was elected as President in 1992. She remained a loyal and hard-working member, graciously handing over the trophies at our annual prize-givings, until the AGM of July 2012, after which she felt unable to continue.

She was a member of the Romantic Novelists Association, and encouraged me to attend meetings in London, and we went together to conferences which took place in University buildings during the summer vacations from 1992 to 2005.

We had more than one garden party at their Dove House Farm in Potter Heigham.

Her husband, Stanley, who sadly predeceased her, had a very quirky sense of humour for a headmaster of Thorpe School, Norwich. He organised one quiz where we had to identify monstrous or down-right odd "ornaments" he had carved and constructed in his garden. One I remember was a yellow "Marigold", which was a rubber washing-up-glove suddenly rising up out of the pond on a pneumatic blast set off by a time-switch.

Olga enjoyed country dancing, and when widowed attended dances with her dancing partner and chauffeur, Charles. Her friends from the group attended her funeral and afterwards performed dances for us, thus making this the jolliest funeral I have ever attended.

Olga embodied in her warmth and humour the aim of the founding members of the Circle, in 1943, "To encourage the art and craft of writing and promote good fellowship amongst Norfolk and Norwich writers generally."

ADJUDICATORS COMMENTS

Alison Bruce

I am obviously looking for writing and compelling stories, but I think you have to adjust the judging to the competition a little bit as well, so for example, I had a story which I liked very much but it briefly mentioned a market in one sentence. As the theme was markets, it was sadly put on the out pile. That's worth considering if you are entering short story competitions. It is not worth getting thrown out for something like that.

I also had a few titles which made me want to read the story, and there were other titles that didn't excite me very much. There was nothing wrong with the short story whatsoever, but it is worth thinking carefully about your titles. You want the reader to be almost engaged from the off and in a couple of cases I was thinking '*oh, okay*'. And others I was thinking I can't wait to read this one, based on the title alone.

Although I don't think that particularly swayed me as far as the short list went, there were a few cases, maybe six, where it was touch and go whether they made it. In other competitions this might make the difference.

A few of the stories were very short, in fact one which has made it into the top ten is quite short but I would say that if you are writing a short story for a competition up to 2,000 words and you are writing one that is only say, 800 words, then it has to be absolutely exceptional to make it. Try and make it 1,800 to 2,000.

Apart from that, I really like a good opening and if you have a really mediocre opening you are on the wrong foot for the reader. But a good opening usually indicates a good story. A bad opening very rarely indicates a good story.

So those were the things I was looking at.

There were probably fourteen that could have made it to the top ten. I tried to make a balance of stories and kept the theme of the market, and different ways of looking at the market theme was quite strong.

Overall I think there were 81 entries. I did judge the short story competition for the Cambridge News some years ago, and I would say that probably at least 80% of your entries were at least the standard of the top ten in the Cambridge competition so generally the standard was very high. I did not mark anyone down for formatting issues at all. I did put comments on some people's story, really because if you are used to reading manuscripts produced in a certain way, it can be distracting when you read something not formatted so well. I pointed this out but did not mark them down.

I read them all through and gave them a rough mark, so I could quickly see who was not at the top of the table, and who was at the bottom. I then slept on it, and when I woke the next day, it was the stories that were still really clear in my mind's eye, were the ones who ultimately got further up. This helped separate them out. When you write it is important to think how certain images are going to stick in the readers' mind. And that was one of the key things that influenced me in the end. Sleeping on it is a top tip.

1st Prize

GUERNICA

by Sue Ryder Richardson

Ana is our grandmother. We call her Lita. She wears black: as if she's a widow. She smells of incense and candle wax. And of oranges.

Lita collects us from school each afternoon. She always takes us to a church and shows us paintings. She tells us of the saints: of how they were martyred. We know it is their suffering that matters. Later, after the holy water, she hands us each a candle. Her pesetas chink into the box. We take the candle to our special saint. I go to San Sebastián. He looks so brave: his white flesh pierced by arrows, his body covered in blood red gashes. My sister always finds Santa Catalina, her name-saint, hers and Lita's sister's. Lita sits in front of the altar. Her rosary clacks as she murmurs her prayers. Always the same quiet prayers, the beads thread their reminder through her fingers.

'You saved your sister's life?' we say one day. 'Mother told us. But that your sister died anyway.'

'Yes. She's dead now.'

'How did you save her?' we ask.

'I'll tell you one day, when you are big girls.' And we walk out into the sunshine to sit on the steps of Santa Eulalia to feed the pigeons.

It seeped out: the story seeped out, over the years. Lita, and our mother, spoke of little things, and we pieced it together. Abu, our grandfather, sat silent. It all happened before his time, and it hurt him to know.

It's Monday. There's no school. There's never school on Mondays: it's market day. Ana is up at five, picking and sorting vegetables. She fills the boxes. Don Pedro, her father, stacks them onto the cart ready for the walk into town. Below, in the valley, they can see the church of Santa Maria. They watch as lights go on, people rise. Sounds echo across the hillside. Farmsteads bristle.

Don Pedro is quiet. He hitches up their donkey, Ella, and takes her bridle. Ella knows every step down to the road, but he needs to take her rein. Times are difficult: he must be in control. Ana walks behind holding Catalina's hand. Their father can be harsh if they step out of line: they tread carefully. Mother sways with the rhythm of the cart. She always sways: to his word, to his needs. She has learned this, learned how avoid his blows. Only she gets to ride.

At the end of the track they meet others: cartloads of produce heading for the square. 'Holas' are muffled. Don Pedro greets few. The girls know not to look up: to seek their classmates' eyes, to recognise their friends. Father says they are all scoundrels: socialists and scoundrels: these Basques.

In the square Ana lays out the produce. It's been her job since she was small. Her tiny hands pile up the tomatoes, peaches, figs, each in their season. Today, she trims lettuces, piles squashes, lays out beans in boxes. She makes a kaleidoscope of colour. Catalina runs back and forth to the cart, bringing each vegetable as Ana calls, until their stall is done. They will sing of its wares all day: their display is important.

Don Pedro crosses the square. From his stride they can sense his displeasure. Ana knows how her arrangement will anger him, it always has. She waits for the clip: across her face, her cheek. It comes, harder than usual. The council has met and a debate raged. It has angered him. The Basques have raised an army against the Nationalists. They will not listen to his voice of reason.

All day he shouts: hollering at the town. The girls serve the customers. They are gentle as they weigh out the produce, put courgettes and onions deep into baskets, place the salad and fruit on top. Their hands take the pesetas and count out change. They smile politeness with their thanks. Across the market Ana watches Luis at his stall: sees him parcel up a cheese into white paper, and hand it to a woman. Ana catches his eye. He points towards the church. She glances at her father, and nods.

'Papa can we go for a break, it's nearly four o'clock?' He nods, 'Take Catalina. Remember. Keep together. No talking to strangers. Here are some pesetas. You've been good girls.' Such praise. So rare.

Ana watches Luis. He slips away, hidden on the further side of the stalls. She knows he's careful: for should Don Pedro see them speak, she would be beaten that night.

They meet in the gardens of Santa Maria: orange blossom perfumes the air. They sit in soft shade, trees filter light over grass, a buttress juts to hide them. Here they can talk. Their hands touch. Luis raises Ana's face and puts his lips to her cheek, he whispers in her ear. His lips move to meet hers, with the fleeting brush of a butterfly wing, he moves across her face.

And it is then that the bell starts to ring. It is loud. The weight of its toll rolls down to them. The warning fills their bodies.

'It won't be here. It'll be Bilbao, again. Don't worry. We'll be fine, I promise.' He holds her tight. Above. The first thrum of a plane comes in on the wind.

'It's only one. It'll pass over. Sit still.' And then there is silence. A breathless stillness, before Ana sees the bombs fall. Six black bombs tumble out of the plane's belly, out of the virgin blue of the sky. She can feel each one. The air stalls. They fall. Then a thunderous blast shatters the town. And the cries start. Screams. And her scream too: it rises from a pit of fear. Luis pulls her to her feet. He pushes her into the church: past the solid stone doorway, into the cool, dark, cavernous church, with its candles and wax and scents. As she peers out, three more planes loom into view, then more and more. There is carnage in the sky.

'Where's Catalina? Papa thinks we're together. I must find her.' She runs out, shrieking her sister's name. But there's no sound, no reply. Only the rush of air as bombs fall, and the roar as they hit the earth.

'Stay here, I'll find her,' Luis commands, and he pulls her back. 'Just stay in the church.'

Outside, an eternity passes. An eternity of screams: the scream of bombs, the screams of people, screams of children, of old, of animals. Roars from men. Inside the church, candles flicker, the eerie half-light is filled with the clacking of rosaries, with murmurations to saints and saviours. Ana strains to hear Luis above the cacophony outside. Then, out of the dust, the flames, and ruins: out of this world of turmoil, Ana sees Luis. He has Catalina by the arm. Her head is thrown back. She roars up at the blackened heavens, just as a sharp ratatatatatata of guns spray the earth

Luis throws Catalina into the church. She lands mired at Ana's feet. Ana hurls herself towards Luis, reaches out her arms to thank him for this miracle. But as she stretches, he flies into the air. A ratatatatatata of bullets pepper his body. A pinprick line of red dots join into a torrent of blood. A red river floods over the dappled grass.

Later, much later, there is silence. A short black, deafening silence. An acute moment of stillness: before the cries and moans and tears begin. Ana reaches Luis. His glazed eyes look up at her. A line of blood runs from his mouth. And she runs, screaming into the market, dragging Catalina through the broken stalls, past the roaring animals, past the mother who cradles a dead baby at her breast, past their vegetables stinking in the burning sun. Past the flames. Past the town. Onto their path home.

Don Pedro has filled the donkey cart. On top, their mother sits, wailing: wanting to wait, to find her girls. She weeps still harder at their return and holds them close.

Don Pedro just shouts at them to get their things. 'We're leaving. The Basques did this. We're going now.'

'But you were saved,' we said one day. We were older then, and had begun to understand. 'You all lived. So why did Catalina die?'

'She died of horror,' said Lita, 'horror and exhaustion.'

She told us then of how they had walked, the four of them, walked south, with the donkey cart, their mother perched on top. She and Catalina beside the wheel as it turned through rutted roads and tracks. They stopped in villages: small towns. In some, Don Pedro found work, until one day he'd come back in a fury. He had fought with someone and hated the town. 'We leave tomorrow,' he'd say.

They journeyed this way for months: short stays, longer stays, old rooms, cramped rooms, always squalor, and always the temper of Don Pedro. They bore it in silence.

It was spring, when they reached Segovia and found a place to settle. But it was too late for Catalina: the journey had exhausted her. Her decline was rapid and she died in their small flat. Lita said she had been ready to go, had longed to die. Catalina had told her that all she could see as she lay on her bed was the wheel that had gone round and round beside her, hour after hour, day after day. And, just like Santa Catalina, death would be a relief.

Their mother died three weeks later. Of grief. The walls of Segovia had become her prison: their father's temper her captor. Lita buried them together in the Iglesia de El Salvador. And left.

And now, at last, Abu, their grandfather, spoke. This was his time: his story. He had listened to Lita's past for many years, had waited outside countless churches as she said her rosary. Now we were to hear his part.

'Every day I saw her. She worked with such care. Setting out the fruit and vegetables in the Calle Buendia. I walked past her on my way to work. She was so young: so fragile. She always wore black. She never spoke. Sometimes she looked up. Her eyes were dark: they looked at me with the sorrow of a nation. There were no tears, just a deep sadness that I longed to take away.'

'So, Abu, you married her?'

'No. Not then, I couldn't. She lived in a room above the shop. The owners loved her like a daughter. They told me she would have to be of age before I could ask.'

'And then I said 'Yes',' Lita laughed: a rare laugh. 'And we had your mother and now both of you. We have been blessed.'

It was later that same week, when their story had finally been told, when Abu had joined Lita in her past: that the picture came.

'It's in Madrid,' Lita told us one morning. 'I will show you the painting of my town: of my story. I have waited so many years for this.'

The queue outside the Prado, snaked in the early autumn heat. People chatted: their memories exposed.

'I was there,' Lita murmured to a man. We followed behind them to the entrance and heard him say: 'This lady is from Guernica. She was in the market. Let her in. Now. Please.'

Inside the gallery the air was cool. It smelled of polish and old dust and sweet lilies. The picture was alone in a long room. It was vast. Lita sat, silent, on a bench,

'There's no market?' I said

'No,' she said, 'But. It is all there.'

'It's all in black and white. There's no colour.'

She sat for a long time, her rosary threaded through her fingers. 'No,' she said, finally.

'There is no red that is red enough to show the blood spilled that day.'

2nd Prize

SCARLETT JOHANNSON IS THE ANTI-CHRIST!

by Louise Wilford

...Coxes ranged in waxy stacks; clementines, pocked spheres balanced in precarious pyramids; green-fingered hands of bananas hanging like claws from hooks snarled in the ceiling net...

Jenny dragged me off down the market this morning. As if I haven't got better things to do than stare at oranges. That's what I said to her:

'You can stuff it, Jen. I've got better things to do!'

'What?' she said. 'What better things?'

I just rolled my eyes at her.

They all think, because you're a teenager you spend your time with your brain on screen save. As if what they do is so much better! Cleaning the microwave and vacuuming the lampshades, that's what mum was doing this morning. And Jenny spent an hour in her bedroom painting her nails Spiced Plum and reading one of her romances.

I mean, who're they to tell me I'm wasting my life?

Anyway, she kept on and on and I could see mum was getting nettled. They'd planned it between them, actually. I heard them in the hall when they thought I was in the kitchen.

'Take her off down the market, Jen,' I heard mum say. 'You two used to go down there every weekend when your Uncle Tone had that fruit and veg stall.' [Mum, I worked there, duh!] 'See if you can't have a chat, sort her out. She might listen to you. God knows, she won't listen to me.'

Well, that's because you talk crap, mum.

The real joke is, it's me they treat like I'm Miss Invisible, not her. O, everyone knows she's there. She never lets people forget. If she's not nagging me and Jen, she's shouting at dad or gossiping with the neighbours or having one of her get-togethers with her mates, when they come over for a Nespresso and slag each other off.

Who is she to give me advice?

Doesn't stop her though, does it? Take last night for instance: 'Luce, why don't we go down the pictures? We could get a big tub of popcorn like we used to. We could watch that new Scarlett Johannson film that's just come out. Your Uncle Tone used to say you looked just like her. Everyone likes Scarlett Johannson, don't they?'

Not me, mum. I think Scarlett Johannson is the

anti-Christ. That's what I said to her. In fact, I shouted it: 'SCARLETT JOHANNSON IS THE ANTI-CHRIST!' Too perfect by half with her blonde hair and little girl mouth and that skinny little body. She makes me want to barf.

...sea-scented carrots, dry gnarled sticks piled, carrot upon carrot, up tight against the swedes; then yellow, knotted, dirty old turnips; sausage stench of bayleaf and basil, purple sage and thyme...

Anyway, mum only wanted me to go to the cinema so she could ply me with snacks. She must think I've got fat in my skull as well as everywhere else. Maybe I have. Fat instead of brains. Her and Jen, discussing me behind my back, like I'm their secret project. They think I can't hear them, but being a teenager doesn't make you deaf. I just wish they'd leave me alone.

But that'd be too simple, wouldn't it, leaving Lucy alone? Your mates are always telling you that you should try new things, so why not give it a go, eh, mum? But, no, it's all 'Take her down the market, Jen, to watch the fruit and veg...'. God, they're both so transparent.

In the end, I just went along with it.

'Whatever,' I said.

I think they could tell I wasn't enthusiastic cos I saw mum roll her eyes at Jen when she thought I wasn't looking.

...Filthy vegetables heaped carelessly in baskets,

on trestle tables, on trolleys, spilling from the backs of parked vans – sweet potatoes, like broken bits of old log, shouldering up to bulbous mottled broccoli and shabby brown-capped mushrooms...

So, anyway, we're here, wandering about between the stalls like a couple of dorks. All Jen needs is a plastic shopping bag over her arm, and she'd really look the part. O, I know she's all dolled up with her plum-coloured nails and raspberry-crush lip gloss, but underneath she was born 55.

God, I hate this bloody place. Uncle Tone used to have his stall upstairs. He's mum's brother, went off to live at the seaside with his wife, Auntie Doris, two years ago. I used to work for him on Saturdays. There was sawdust on the floor at the back. He liked to show off the tattoo on his forearm – an anchor with the name LUCY on it. He'd make a big thing of it, because Lucy's my name too. But obviously his tattoo wasn't done for me – he had it done years ago when he was in the navy, in memory of some girl he knew. Not Auntie Doris, obviously. Some earlier girl. He used to say I reminded him of her. Her and Scarlett Johannson.

Uncle Tone thought he was God's Gift – mum always said he could charm the birds off the trees, but he never charmed me. He used to run his hand up the back of my thigh, under my skirt, when I leaned over to bag up the veg.

Why is it so hard, Leaving Lucy Alone?

...blinding smell of leeks and purple onions, raw

variegated globes staring after you as you walk away...

Jen has spotted a jewellery stall. She might be a saddo but she has got this thing about body piercing. It's her one saving grace. She's had her ears pierced three times – each of them has a curve of glossy studs in different colours – red, orange, green, like traffic lights. They're nice. And she's got her belly button done too. She wears these little crop tops to show it off. She's got a fancy new pin in it today with a little jointed lizard hanging down towards her groin – it jiggles about when she moves, little slithery movements so it looks like its climbing up her abdomen. It's pretty cool really. But gross too.

She wants me to have mine done, but there's no chance. No sweaty geezer in a vest, with tattoos down both arms, is going to stick a bloody great needle through my stomach. Jen starts doing her cajoling act:

'Luce, it don't hurt. It's over in a split second. You'll hardly notice.'

No, like you didn't when it swelled up and you had to keep swabbing it down with Dettol and dad was talking about going to A & E? Duh.

'I'm too fat.'

'How many times? You've got a stomach like a bread board – in fact it goes in, not out. It's called body dysmorphia, Luce – I've read about it.'

This is Jen's thing, using fancy words she finds on

the internet and talking to me like she's an expert. She left school at sixteen – she didn't even try to do A Levels. But she talks to me like I'm the idiot.

And then I find I'm edging away, turning, walking off with quickening steps, almost jogging, dodging round people. So many people. Everywhere you turn, there's more of them, stallholders shouting at you, little kids running round waving stuff at you, old biddies trying to trip you up with their shopping baskets on wheels. And the fruit and veg stalls, smelling like a kick in the face.

I can feel the sawdust on the back of my legs.

And Jen is scuttling after me, grabbing my arm. 'Where you going, Luce? Look, if you don't want your belly button done, that's okay. Let's go up to Renshaws sweets, eh, and get a pound of peanut brittle for dad. He'll be back tonight. We can surprise him.'

Oh yeah, I think, bet he'll be dead thrilled by a bag of peanut brittle off the market! Make his day, that will. Still, what can he expect? He's never here, always off somewhere, selling drugs. Legally, I mean. He works for a drug company. Mum always jokes about it to people. 'My husband sells drugs!' She thinks it's funny.

But at least she's around. More's the pity. It'd be better if she went off selling drugs to doctors and pharmacies and hospitals, driving off to all those places - Acrington, Middlesbrough, Luton - and he stayed with us. He's a good cook. He used to cook a lot years ago, before he got this job: chilli, curry – he likes spicy food. He used to make a fantastic shepherd's pie with baked beans and smoked paprika, his own recipe. That was when I still ate things, before I realised I was so fat.

Mum can't cook to save her life.

Dad must hate all that driving round, hardly ever seeing us. He always looks so tired, when he does come home. So sad. And mum doesn't help – always nagging him, niggling, making sarky remarks. And all he gets from us is a bag of peanut brittle!

God, them fruit and veg stalls don't half stink.

...Pale squashes rising obscenely from green plastic trays; bruised tomatoes in slurping puddles; cucumber truncheons about to cosh unwary lettuces...

'Come on, Luce. Renshaws is up here!'

As if I don't know. I used to come here every Saturday, helping load up the stall in the early morning, serving customers. Uncle Tone's stall was right next to Renshaws. I used to buy sweets from Renshaws sometimes, before I realised how fat I was getting. Before I stopped eating.

We move away, Jen and I, up to the second level of the indoor market, towards the sweet stall. It's more of a permanent booth, covered with a stripy awning. Someone else runs it now.

I remember brushing sawdust off the back of my t-shirt.

'...It don't hurt, love! I'd never hurt you. It'll be

over soon. You'll enjoy it. You girls always do. God, you don't half remind me of Scarlett Johannson. If you lost half a stone, you'd be a dead ringer...'

And that's when it happens. Jen is gazing at the assortment of different sweets in clear plastic jars, as if she's trying to choose a library book. And I'm looking vaguely at the trays of sweets they've arranged in a row down one side of the booth, each with a plastic scoop. One tray's full of chocolate buttons, white and milk, coated in hundreds and thousands, masses of them, surrounded by tiny grains of pastel-coloured shrapnel where they've broken or the candy's been knocked off. Then there's a tray of cinder toffee, like bits of old wood, all different sizes; some of it's been overcooked and is darker, shrivelled, melted round the edges. And there's jelly babies, like unformed foetuses, suffocating in icing sugar, all jumbled together, upside down, standing on their heads, lying on their backs like corpses – one red one's been squashed against the tray and looks like roadkill.

And suddenly I can't stand it any more. I can't stand them all looking at me, wanting me to stuff them in my mouth, calling to me, colours colliding, scents all muddled up, like mud in a swamp – harem smells, chocolate and sugar and ginger and vanilla and mint – garish colours sizzling into the background blur of noise and movement.

I can't stand them all hammering inside my head.

'Luce, Luce, what you doing?'

I'm tipping up the trays, spilling the stuff out across the floor, where it mixes with the sawdust, kicking it, stamping on it. I can see a woman pulling her little boy back, away from me – an old bloke with a stick staring at me with disapproving horror – the stallholder moving towards me with a determined expression on her jowly face.

'Hey, you'll have to pay for that lot, missy!'

And Jen, staring, staring at me as if I've killed someone, as if I've finally flipped.

Which I have.

I've finally, finally, flipped.

3rd Prize

CIRCLE OF LIFE

by Rhona Godfrey

It's her again: light-fingered Lily. My name for her, because she seems to favour floral-themed items to steal. And her cream coloured skin and dark-red hair somehow make me think of lilies. She comes to my stall then something else goes...

The season opened in April and I remember looking at her, but there were a lot of people browsing that morning. I noticed later that a silver ring with a 'daisy' motif had disappeared, but I couldn't remember who'd been at the stall that day.

The first Saturday in May was a gloriously sunny day and the public had ventured out in appreciation of it. All the stalls were busy, especially the food stalls, which had hungry queues. My mouth watered at the aromas wafting by: roasting meats, garlic, coffee, herbs...

She was there again, at the edge of my stall, gently separating the chains of pendants as if searching for something special. She looked different, somehow -

maybe just tired.

'Want a hand at all?' I asked, hopefully.

'Just looking, thanks.' she replied, smiling gently. I wanted to get a conversation going but someone else asked me where the public toilets were. When I looked again she was gone, and I felt disappointed. When I packed everything up in the afternoon, I couldn't see a pendant I'd made. I was proud of it: it had been one of my first efforts. A poppy design: silver with red enamelled petals and tiny silver anthers at the centre. It was then that I began to wonder about her...

June came, and I had almost forgotten 'Lily' until she appeared just before noon. I nodded a welcome to her and she smiled in return, but I could see she looked strained, anxious. Before I got a chance to speak to her, a woman on my right started asking me about my jewellery. Did I make all the jewellery myself? (Yes – apart from the chains). Were all the stones real ones or glass? I bristled a bit at that: I'd spent a long time sourcing the stones. Garnets are my own favourite, the colour of blood and wine. I like using silver for its coolness and its calming feel. And I like creating things using themes from nature: trees, birds, flowers, sun, moon and stars.

The customer chose a pair of amethyst drop earrings and wandered off again. I then had time to register Lily's absence - also the absence of a silver bangle, which had been on the end of a velvet-covered display stand. I'd made it during the winter, spending hours painstakingly engraving a design of convolvulus flowers with leaves and twining stems on it.

I started to feel angry, now. The items she'd taken weren't of huge financial value but they were labours of love. I'd done a silversmithing course at the local college and had spent a lot of my savings on materials and tools before starting to create jeweller to sell. To me, they were works of art, which I hoped would be appreciated as such, as well as bringing in money.

The monthly market stall rent was an expense and my profits were hardly impressive.

Now this young woman believed she could just come along each month and choose herself something free of charge? She might be lovely to look at, but plainly she lacked something in the 'morals' department. I determined to set a trap for her - for July's market.

So here we are: it's the first Saturday in July. The weather doesn't seem to know it's supposed to be summer: it's grey and windy. The town's shops rather than the market are drawing the customers today. We're quiet, apart from food stalls where early-morning regulars are shopping for farmhouse bread, locally-grown fruit and veg, and cheeses neatly wrapped in blue and white paper. 'Shopping' box ticked: that's the rest of Saturday free.

I've set my trap. Lily's already taken a ring, pendant and bracelet from me. Will she want something different, or more of the same? I've laid out tempting floral offerings in prominent display. Dave, at the adjoining stall (handcrafted leather goods) has been briefed on the situation and will be keeping an eye out as a witness if needed.

'Hey, Norrie – I might have to manhandle her a bit, just to warn you!' I grin at his joke but don't like to think of him getting too close to Lily.

The morning drags due to lack of customers. I start to feel both disappointed yet also relieved. The truth is - although I don't like being ripped-off, I'm trying not to think about what happens after you catch a shoplifter – a scuffle, tears, people staring, the police? I dread the idea of any of that. Just when I'm about to give up and ask Dave to watch both stalls in return for venison burgers all round - thar she blows…!

Today, she's wearing jeans and a dark-coloured top, with some lacy scarf-thing around her neck as a nod to the windy day. Her hair, previously wound up into some intricate tower on the back of her head involving chopsticks or some other heathen thing, is today dragged back carelessly into a ponytail. The wind lifts its flame-like strands. I catch myself examining her, noticing that she looks wearier than the last time. I tell myself to man-up and focus on not losing any more of my goods to her.

She comes directly over to me. 'Hi there!' I say - with great originality: I was nervous. She replies, 'I've come to pay for the things I've taken and I'm really sorry I did it.'

Now, I'm not au fait with this kind of situation: I

gawp at her. She holds her hand out.

'Is fifty quid enough?'

'More than enough,' I say, taking it. I turn to find change, but when I look back she's vanishing through the small crowd gathered around the roast chicken stall. Dave and I just look at each other: bewildered. I wonder why she did it, what made her pay me back? It's all a mystery, and I wish I knew the answers.

She didn't return in August or September and the season's now over till April. My Saturdays are my own again, and the job I have in the bookshop four days a week will keep me going as long as I'm careful.

At the start of October, I head in to town to get some shopping myself. It's a sharp, cold sunny day, with brilliant white clouds scudding along. There's a pleasant smell of garden waste bonfires: almost like incense. I treat myself to a blue wool sweater, since my beloved elderly one has been got-at by moths since last winter. Then I go for a coffee in 'Bean Good', spreading my newspaper across the shelf table at the window. I can watch the world go by while attempting to complete today's Quick Crossword.

I become aware of someone standing beside me, and I look up. It's Lily! Smiling warily, she says, 'Alright if I sit here?' I make three different responses at once and it comes out as a kind of croak. She sets her coffee down and I wait to see what's next.

'Norrie – that's your name isn't it? I saw it on your

business cards on the stall. I'm sorry about what I did.'

I start to make 'Oh, don't worry…' noises, but she keeps talking.

'I wanted to explain it, but it took all my courage to turn up like that, with the money. I was scared you'd be angry. I took these things because I couldn't afford to pay for them, and I wanted to have them for my mum.'

She gulped a mouthful of coffee: too hot, so I waited till she spoke again. 'Mum was diagnosed with cancer last year and I gave up my job to go home and look after her. I wanted to give her things to make her happy while it was still possible. She loved flowers but she couldn't get out any more, and it was hard to see her fading away in the spring while everything else was starting to bloom. So I picked wildflowers, twigs with leaf-buds opening, flowers from the Botanic Gardens…'

Lily looked at me ruefully at that point, then resumed: 'When I saw your stall with the beautiful jewellery you make, I wanted so much to get something for her. But I was broke since I'd had to stop work. It was a rotten thing to do: stealing from you, but I promised myself I would pay you back some day so that helped me manage to do it.'

'And you did come back and pay, so that's fine with me.' I said, firmly. I could see she was upset and I believed that her remorse was genuine.

She swallowed, and glanced out the window. 'Mum died in June. I managed to get my old job back because my boss knew Mum. So I have money again, at least.'

'I'm sorry about your Mum,' I said, meaning it. 'And I'm sorry I won't have a chance to meet her, she sounds lovely'.

'Thank you,' she replied. 'If you want to, you can meet me now: properly, this time.' She smiled at me: 'I'm Rose.'

Of course you are, I thought to myself - grinning in an idiotic manner. 'Pleased to meet you!'

It's now the end of March and I have to get ready for the first market of the season. The weather could be better: heavy rain's going on and off as if someone's flicking a switch. It's a bit early for flowers, but I've been working in secret on a silver ring: set in its wide band it has a rose made up of little garnets – the colour of love. It should fit her well, I hope.

EL RASTRO

by April McIntyre

The net caught in my nails as I stretched to hook it to an overhead branch. The heat at midday was like a ceramicists kiln, dry and suffocating, even in November. I turned to see the net coming together nicely, the others scrambling to attach it to neighbouring branches before lifting up their cañas, then – whack. The olives rained down, light little thumps as they hit the net and rolled to a stop. Careful not to damage the branches, we swung our cañas lightly.

Eventually you'd develop "the knack" and could delicately hit the olives out of the tree whilst keeping all the leaves and branches intact. Any leaves that we did collect went into teas, a taste that one must acquire over many weeks. Over the following months the air on the farm began to thicken and after a short winter, where the smell of smoke permeated everything as farmers began burning branches, the sweltering heat of July finally hit.

A pale, marginally overweight woman in her twenties only months before, I looked at myself in the mirror hanging loosely on the wall of my casita. My skin, the colour of light dirt, my body firmer and stronger than before. I heard the faint trot of Olivia, the farm cat, who had taken it upon herself to be my vicious protector and followed me everywhere. Her tail poker-straight, pointing towards the cloudless sky as she followed me towards the top garden.

The sun gave no respite to the garden at the highest point of the farm. Perfect for tomatoes. I set a large plastic bucket down by the vines as Olivia tucked herself under a nearby tree. I started with my favourites; Corazón de Cabrito, and then the delicate yellow pear-shaped tomatoes, which were perfectly sweet and addictive. I pocketed a few for dinner. Laden with a basket of vibrant red and yellows, I whistled to Olivia and negotiated the narrow, dusty path to the house.

My casita was essentially a mud hut. Inside there stood a wood burner and a small kitchen-cum-bedroom and my bed was a mattress laid upon two wooden pallets. There were grape vines covering the front of the house and a kiwi twisted itself around the pergola to the side of the building.

'Looking good,' Lourdes said, as she greeted me at the house. I followed her into the kitchen.

'Yeah, we've got a good load this month, these Corazóns' should pick us up a few euro and the fig jam is beautiful.' I put the bucket with the rest of the produce that had begun to take over my kitchen.

'How are we doing for eggs? Cheese?' Lourdes inquired, peeking inside the cloth-covered boxes.

'Cheese needs two more turns, and the eggs are coming thick and fast, the girls have us covered. They're laying like crazy.'

'Perfect.' I always felt so proud when Lourdes was happy. She rarely smiled and when she did I felt like I'd accomplished something great.

The farm sat in a rural Andalucían valley, about an hour away from Granada. Olives and their oil were the main income as well as almonds. I'd arrived twelve months before as an excuse to escape a life that had worn me down to nothing. Now I dreamt of carrots instead contracts, spent hours each evening watering the gardens instead of losing nights staring at my laptop. It took me a week to stop missing the internet and a little longer to stop missing real toilets. Any trip to the local town was a chance to shit in a proper toilet, in private. Apart from that, life on the farm suited me. Volunteers, hitchhikers and locals came and went and each week was full of new stories and languages.

It was a peacefulness I had never experienced before and something I wasn't ready to give up any time soon. Everything took a long time. Cooking, done over an open fire, food grown from seed, and weeding; there was always weeding.

On the night before the rastro – a monthly market run by locals and a handful of British hippies – I loaded the van for the early start. There was no road into the farm so each box and bag and bucket needed to be carried up a steep dirt path, it's roots; often the cause of twisted ankles and bashed knees.

I knew the roots and stones by heart now and barely looked towards the ground while walking. Olivia followed. The path led to a small stucco village where packs of stray dogs kept us all on our toes. Lourdes had no sympathy for the mangy pack animals anymore and often threw stones when they came near. I was still used to dogs being pets.

'Giann will come and help tomorrow', Lourdes informed me. Giann was a new volunteer who specialised in arboriculture. I hadn't spoken to him much, he was from Somerset and played guitar. That's all I knew.

'Great.' It had just been Lourdes and I at the rastro the last few months and that's how I liked it. I tried not to let the disappointment touch my voice.

Lourdes let out an exhausted sigh and wiped her head on her sleeve.

'That's it. Get some sleep. We'll meet here at five.'

'Hasta mañana.' I headed back down to the farm.

The sun was just setting so I raced to part of the farm that overlooked the valley below. The imposing dark mound of Sierra Lugar ahead, was cast with pinks and oranges on its east face as the sun turned the sky into a palette of pastels.

It was the only time the air was cool. I sank into an old wicker chair that had been there since I arrived. The view was enough to entertain anyone who hadn't watched TV in nearly a year. I often sat there until it was dark and the cicadas started their songs.

My head lolled as Lourdes bounded along the

small dirt road towards town. We stopped twice to pick up hitchhikers. Lourdes would always stop if she had room. Most of the people we picked up were usually hitching into town from the commune in the nearby hills.

Giann was crammed in the back with the two strangers, their hair, both nests of mangled dreadlocks. His lap was piled with boxes of lemons, avocados and prickly pears. He gave me a goofy smile. His eyes were dark; I think I remembered him saying something about his father being Greek. He tied his trousers around his waist with a piece of string.

The rastro was bustling and there was always a sense of urgency and anxiety in the air as vendors unloaded their vans and tried to get the best spot. Lourdes knew most of them by name and I was becoming a more familiar sight to the sellers there who smiled and nodded as I flipped open the table's A-frame legs.

'I've got it.' Giann picked up the table.

'No, it's fine. I do this on my own all the time,' I snapped. 'Sorry, I mean, why don't you take the brined olives and put a couple of small tasting bowls out?' I recovered.

'Of course.' Giann smiled, with a small nod of acceptance.

A small van pulled up next to us with Spanish prog-rock blaring through the windows. Lourdes smiled and ran over to open the door. A small, tanned woman hopped out and kissed her before she opened the boot. They spoke in Spanish, then

Lourdes brought her over.

'This is my partner, Camila,' she said beaming.

I'd never met Camila but Lourdes spoke of her often. She was a teacher and part-time potter.

After the introductions, Giann and I unloaded some pottery from Camila's van and set it up next to our stall.

'You think you can handle one stand each?' Lourdes asked, dusting insects off the lemons. 'Camila and I need to take one of the burras to the vets and considering there's two of you, now might be the best time to get her in.'

'Sure,' we said in unison.

Lourdes and Camila waved as they drove off.

The rastro was loud and buzzing as always. I had spent the previous day making bread, which I'd laid out in baskets upon gingham cloths. We had bottles of our oil, vegetables, chutneys, almonds and jams. The peppery smell of the oil hit my nostrils, I remember milling it in January and sticking my finger beneath the silver spout to taste it. It was the smell of Andalucía. A mobile bar turned up selling beer and tortilla. People began to fill in and the market started to come to life.

'Wow, this is really something,' Giann shouted over the locals handing him money for bread and jam.

I smiled and nodded, at least he was working hard. The customers seemed to like his floppy hair and lyrical West Country accent.

'Yeah it's pretty hectic.' I bagged two bottles of

olive oil and some avocados as Paco from the bar placed a cold beer in front of me. I looked at him as if he'd just saved my life. 'Muchas gracias,' I thanked him profusely.

There was a short lull and I took the opportunity to take a look at what others were selling. A lot of the people from the commune would be selling bread and cakes. Some locals had tables stacked with children's board games and old VHS tapes. I picked up a pasty filled with goats' cheese and honey, a hand-knitted winter hat and some cheese from a village up in the mountains. Vendors had tied sheets to large poles to shade themselves, creating a multi-coloured ocean of billowing sheets. People would begin drinking early and carry on late into evening. The sun seemed to make everybody friendly, drunk and happy. It was less about buying and more about socialising for the locals, who sat beneath umbrellas smoking and nursing bottles of Alhambra Reserva.

The day went on and the avocados began to wrinkle under the blistering heat. The tomatoes and other salad vegetables were sold and only one bottle of oil remained. Camila's pots had done well with only a few small, hand-painted bowls left. I felt parched, and realised I had barely had anything to drink all day. I looked down to see my warm, flat beer.

'I'll get you another,' Giann said, heading to the bar.

We sat up on a wall behind the stand. Our legs

dangling. Giann was tall, his thin legs ending with worn out sandals. How many places had they been I wondered. We finished our beers and set to packing up. I could see Lourdes chatting to some locals in the car park. I waved, signalling that we were ready to load the van.

'That was fun,' Giann, said as he helped me lift the boxes into the back.

I smiled.

After we unloaded the leftovers back at the farm I was exhausted. Olivia was waiting for me outside my door. I picked her up, which she hated, but she let me for a second until she wriggled away. I walked over to the alberca at the side of the house and splashed my face.

Back overlooking the valley in front of Sierra Lugars rocky façade, I relaxed into the chair. My bare feet were swollen from the heat. I let the faint breeze cool and unwind each ligament with a stroke of air. The black cat curled herself up under my seat and I could hear Giann playing his guitar from his casita farther down the valley. I put my hand in my pocket and pulled out the three yellow tomatoes I had stuffed in there two days before and forgotten about. They still tasted sweet.

Tonight I will dream of carrots, I thought.

FADING TIMES

by Kathy Joy

Iris pulled her battered wooden trunk behind her down the high street. The wheels at the back were worn but sturdy as she navigated the uneven pavement until she reached her stall on the market. It took her longer than usual to set up the tables and lay out her wares. It was getting worse. Lifting her hand, Iris studied the way her hands faded around the edges, especially at her fingertips. How long did she have?

Opposite was a stall called 'PJ's'. It sold pyjamas and night dresses but also offered tracksuits and other comfortable clothing options. Not so long ago it had taken up two units. Now it had been crammed into one.

Iris remembered when the market was the heart of the community, with customers passing through every day like blood cells through an artery. Vendors came from around the world to trade, fighting each other for position, and people flocked to see the latest wares. Now, less than half the units were occupied, and customers were fleeting.

A woman cut across the road, making a beeline for Iris' stall. This was promising.

Iris smiled and greeted the woman, but was ignored. Instead, the woman was fixated on her stock. When had people gotten so rude that they couldn't manage a simple greeting?

'This,' the woman said, pointing to a porcelain teapot, the sides painted with intricate smoke-like swirls. 'How much is it?'

Iris gave the woman the usual up and down. People gave away much without realising. There were bags under her eyes, and she had worn calloused hands. Freshly lacquered nails and thick make-up failed to hide fatigue.

The teapot wasn't meant for this customer. No, this woman was overworked but still eager to please. Her many responsibilities were weighing her down. Iris knew she had just the item for her. Stepping closer, sending her long skirt swirling about her legs, Iris plucked a hat from a stand.

'Perhaps this would suit you better?' Iris held the item out, maintaining eye contact.

The woman hesitated. 'No... it's for my daughter. She's into all this new age stuff.'

'But you work so hard. Don't you think you deserve something nice? Something just for you?' Iris chanced a step closer.

The woman stared at the hat. She liked it, that was certain. For a moment Iris thought she had finally snagged a customer, the woman's fingers a hairsbreadth from the item, but then she snapped her gaze back to the teapot. 'Look, I haven't got time for this upselling nonsense. I want the teapot and nothing else. How much is it?'

When Iris failed to answer immediately, the woman whipped out her phone. For a moment, both stood silently as Iris wasn't quite sure what to say or do. She had never liked mobile phones. They had their uses, but these days' people relied on them too much. Their faces were glued to screens.

'Never mind, I've found it online. Probably cheaper too.' The woman spun on her heel without so much as a goodbye.

Iris almost doubled over in pain, feeling a large chunk of her centre fade. Rechecking her hand she saw a finger was missing. After taking several deep breaths, she straightened and stepped out of her stall to assess how busy it was.

At the end of the row, an elderly stallholder was sticking sale signs on the walls and stock. Iris recognised him. His name was Gareth. Many years ago, Iris had returned to this market and held a stall beside him. Gareth was just a boy then, hurriedly following his father's barked orders as they set up the stall every morning. Back then it sold shoes, but it had evolved and now specialised in all-weather gear, including hiking boots. Gareth raised his hand in a wave, which Iris returned.

An hour went by, then another. Still no customers. At this rate, Iris might not make it to the end of the day. What then? Famine, pestilence, civil unrest, the industrial revolution and both world wars had come and gone, and Iris and her trunk had survived it all. Now, like the market, she was slowly vanishing. Her fate was tied to it.

It wasn't just here, either. Iris travelled the country and had seen Blackbushe shrivel and die along with many others. Even Portobello Road was starting to slump despite its best efforts.

Seeing it happen here hurt most. Iris had been born in this city. Starving and alone, she had tried to steal from a market stall only to be caught. Rather than handing her over to the law, the owner took her on as an apprentice and taught her the magic in each item, how to read people and figure out just what they needed. Iris had watched thousands of stories play out, some good, some bad. A down on his luck man was given a pocket watch, and within a few months, he became mayor. A young widow given a red hair ribbon was found floating in the river days later. She had not survived her trial.

Iris and her predecessor did not sell cursed items. Those who did were quickly rooted out and chased from town – or worse, hanged. Instead, Iris' pieces attracted the attention of the Fates. Customers faced demanding trials, but if they succeeded, they received fate's favour.

A crowd gathered around Gareth's stall, the customers clamouring, picking the inventory clean like vultures around a fresh kill. Iris tried to lure some over, but they paid her no heed, hypnotised by the bright discount signs.

After a few hours, a woman broke through the

congregation, her heels clacking against the pavement as she marched determinedly towards Iris. Behind her, a small army of cats followed. Iris recognised her – she always recognised past customers, whether they were recent or from long ago.

'You!' She pointed at Iris as she drew near.

'Welcome back, Madam. How may I help you?'

'I don't know what you've put in this thing, but ever since I put it on, cats have been following me everywhere. Is this some kind of prank?' The woman stepped away as a cat tried to rub against her leg. She reached around to the silver necklace in the shape of a cat with twinkling amber eyes resting against her chest. 'The damn thing won't come off. I've even tried cutting it. Get it off me, or I swear I'll tell everyone about your cursed things.'

Iris smiled. 'I do not sell cursed items. I sell opportunities. If you…'

'Oh cut that voodoo crap and get it off. Now.'

Iris leaned forward, touched the clasp, and it popped open. The necklace slid away from the woman's neck and into Iris' hand. In an instant, the cats dispersed.

The woman wheeled on Iris. 'I knew it was you. How dare you.' Red stole up her cheeks, making her round face look like a wrinkled tomato. 'You had better compensate me.'

'Compensate you?'

'I demand money for the emotional trauma you've put me through!'

'You didn't pay for the item. There is no refund.

You've given up your opportunity and are back to where you were before, no better, no worse.'

The woman continued to bluster, hurling abuse, but Iris paid it no heed. She was far from the first angry customer Iris had dealt with, though lately, she'd been getting more than she used to.

'Just you wait! I know my rights! The customer is always right!' The woman spat finally before stomping away.

Quiet returned to the market. The odd customer hovered in from time to time, but none ventured across the threshold. Every hour that ticked by felt like a weight pressing down on Iris as the strength poured from her body.

What had happened to the world?

Watching people mill along the streets, faces in their phones, headphones jammed in their ears, she realised it wasn't the world that had changed – it was the people.

Nobody wanted to deal with hardship anymore, even if they knew it would lead to something good. They wanted the quick and the easy. They shopped online, hunting for bigger and better deals, or ways to make money with minimal effort. Worse, customers seemed to believe they were entitled to preferential treatment and thought they knew better than professionals. They had the option to take their money anywhere, and they held it over vendors like a knife to the throat.

Maybe the shift in power was a good thing, maybe it wasn't. All Iris knew was that it was the end of her livelihood – her very existence.

On more than one occasion Iris had thought about biting the bullet and transferring her business online. She knew several like her who had. The trouble was online customers were just a username or an email. How could she give a string of numbers, letters and symbols the right item? She needed to see a person, to look into their eyes and know them.

Dizziness swelled, hitting her like a wave, dragging her under. This was it. Already she could feel the hollowness of non-existence burrowing at her centre, devouring her from the inside out. The hubbub of other stall holders packing up and the dull buzz of people making their way down the high street surrounded her. Hardly a fitting death knell. Why did it have to end like this?

'Excuse me!' A voice came, cutting through the din. 'Are you still open?'

Iris spun to see a young girl wearing a green dress and a sunhat. She recognised the girl – remembered calling out to her that morning as she powerwalked by, music blaring from her headphones, smart-phone out in front of her.

Taking a deep breath, Iris willed herself to remain for one more second.

'You're sure you wouldn't rather shop online?' Iris spoke, determined to offer one final retort against the darkness that dragged her down.

'I hate shopping online. You don't know who you're buying from. I much prefer talking to a real person and walking away with my stuff.'

A brief burst of strength allowed Iris to straighten and lock eyes with the girl. Part of her foot had faded so she had to hobble towards the table to grab the ring nestled upon a red velvet cushion. 'I'll bet this ring is a perfect fit. Care to try it?'

The girl didn't answer at first. She eyed the ring, then Iris. Desire blossomed across her face. All she had to do was take it.

Just when Iris thought she was going to decline, the girl took the ring and slid it on her thin finger, holding it out, turning it this way and that, marvelling at how the red gemstone burned as it caught the light. The spell was cast.

Silence fell between the two. It seemed for a moment that the girl was going to walk away without another word, but instead, she turned to Iris.

'Do you have a Facebook page?' the girl asked.

Iris shook her head, feeling the weakness begin to return. 'My business doesn't really work online.'

'You can still have a page though. There are plenty of groups who love little stalls like this. Here.' The girl took out her phone and showed Iris the online communities she belonged to. Each comment about wanting more physical shops, protecting small businesses, and cries of 'save our high streets' filled the gaping void until Iris finally had the strength to stand unaided. She listened as the girl offered to help set one up for her and explained in detail how they worked. Stunned, Iris didn't say much. Instead, she lifted her hand, marvelling at her fingertips. They hadn't been this solid in ages.

THE PALE CHILD

by Iain Andrews

'They never told you about the pale child?'

The apothecary leant in as he spoke, his voice hoarse from years of smoking a pipe. He'd sold potions from his booth in the market for longer than anyone could remember.

'And you a butcher?' said the tailor, his features rendered demonic by shadows sculpted by the flames in the hearth. We were seated in one of the taverns that crowded round the ancient square.

'My father is the butcher,' I replied. 'One day I will run his business but for now I only sell his meat.'

The apothecary stared at the fire. 'The child will not care.'

I hoped they were merely making fun of a newcomer. 'Why should I fear a child?'

'Not any child,' muttered the tailor.

The apothecary nodded. 'You have seen him just the once, have you not?'

'Who knows?' I replied. 'Four weeks ago, a mere glimpse. A small figure in rags who stared at me for a full minute before fleeing. No doubt a beggar's son, or some runaway from the workhouse.'

The apothecary pointed the stem of his pipe towards the window. A full moon bathed the deserted market in eerie light. 'He only appears on a night like this. You should pray for clouds before you leave the inn.'

I forced a chuckle. 'Then I shall get wet. And besides, others than I might see him.' I grinned at the tailor. 'Why, perhaps you might find him stalking you tonight.'

The tailor shook his head. 'I am not a butcher.' A malevolent smile creased his face. 'Nor his apprentice.'

Perhaps the ale was taking effect – my nervousness was subsiding. 'I am young and strong. No child can intimidate me. So tell me why I should cower before this infant.'

The tailor and apothecary exchanged hollow laughs. I became convinced they were taking me for a naive fool.

The apothecary bent over and knocked his pipe against the grate. 'First, have you ever noticed that most of your trade is conducted as the sun sets?'

'So what? My customers have ceased their labour for the day. It is obvious they would buy meat on their way home.'

The apothecary shot me a piteous smile. 'If that were true, my own trade would follow suit. It does not, for my own clientele comprises servants and women who reside at home, as does that of the other butchers. Your own stall is not established, but those who hunger for meat will find no other stall open at dusk. The other butchers are long vanished, afraid of the pale child.'

I dismissed his logic as another attempt to scare me. 'Then they are cowards, frightened by a gossip's tale.'

'Do not confuse courage with ignorance,' said the apothecary.

I laughed. 'Then spin me the tale if you wish to see me tremble.'

'Very well.' The apothecary filled his pipe and lit it with a long taper from the fire. 'Many years ago, the city was in turmoil. The countryside was in revolt, and food was scarce. There were four butchers in the market. Three were as honest as a man could expect in your trade, but the other was a known scoundrel.'

'Some say he was in league with the devil,' added the tailor.

'Indeed,' said the apothecary, 'although even Satan himself would have thought twice about entering an alliance with such a man.' He blew a ring of smoke towards the ceiling. 'I believe his stall was on the very same spot yours now occupies. He had taken a mistress, the widow of a murdered candlemaker.'

'Many claim the husband was slain by the butcher,' said the tailor.

The apothecary shrugged. 'Perhaps. We must assume that the lot of a widow in those days was so poor that she had little choice but to serve that evil man. To no-one's surprise, he treated her so harshly that in the end she took her own life.'

The tailor touched me on the arm. 'Filled her pockets with stones and walked into the river.'

The apothecary relit his pipe. 'So they say. She had a child, a boy of perhaps nine or ten. The butcher's cruelty did not stop at the mother. He kept the child chained in the space below his counter, only releasing the boy for long enough to steal from his rivals.'

'You see,' said the tailor, 'only a child could crawl in the voids beneath the stalls. The boy would seize meat from the shelves then disappear into the darkness beneath.'

'Why did the child not try to escape?' I asked.

'He knew no other life,' replied the tailor, 'even though he must have hated the butcher.'

The apothecary shivered as he glanced at the moon. 'No-one suspected at first. Times were hard, and an urchin stealing from the market was commonplace. The child was feral, a grotesque figure with long unkempt hair and fingernails like a dragon's claws.'

The tailor resumed their tale. 'Such a creature could not remain hidden forever. He was seen by one of his victims, who struck the fleeing boy with a cleaver, rendering the child's left arm useless.'

'So you see,' said the apothecary, 'why the child seeks revenge on those who trade in meat.'

I remained sceptical. 'You speak of a time long past. The boy must have died centuries ago.'

'Indeed.' The apothecary sucked on his pipe. 'The child was last seen alive a week after his injury. Another butcher almost caught him. The boy was now a liability.'

Their story was intriguing, I granted them that. 'Did the evil butcher kill the boy, then?'

The tailor laughed. 'Who knows? The body was never found, but how easy is it for a butcher to dispose of a corpse?'

'But not a vengeful spirit,' said the apothecary. 'The butcher was found three months later, lying dead before his stall, a look of terror etched upon his face. Three months, mark you well.'

'So?' I refused to be seen as a fool. 'A footpad, a failure of the heart... More likely explanations than a ghost.'

The apothecary pointed the stem of his pipe directly towards me. 'Three months. And under six months later the man who wounded the child was found dead, his throat ripped apart. Perhaps clouds kept him alive a little longer. They say the boy appears twice at the time of a bright full moon. Those who meet him for the third time will perish.'

'Show me your evidence.'

'Seek it yourself,' snapped the tailor. 'Ask the other tradesmen. Walk among the tombstones in the churchyard.'

I bade them a contemptuous farewell and sought the fellowship of more convivial companions. I was unaccustomed to strong ale, and was in a merry mood when I left the tavern. Desiring to reach my home as quickly as possible, I walked between the deserted market stalls.

A child blocked my way.

He was small, his hair long and matted. One arm hung limp by his side, the other extended as if he was pointing with the long curved nail that extended from his bony finger. Even at fifteen paces, a smell reminiscent of a charnel house wafted towards me. Although he seemed frail, I confess I was scared and turned to leave the market by another exit.

The boy stood in my way once more. The brilliance of the moon was behind him, and I swear his body was translucent, allowing the silver light to illuminate his thin body. Now he was pointing directly towards me, that terrible claw aimed at my heart.

I ran. Left or right, backwards or forwards, I could not escape that fiendish creature. It was ten minutes before I found myself quivering and breathless by the church wall that borders the market. I saw no more of the pale child that night.

I was reluctant to return to my work the next day, but in the light of dawn my father's wrath seemed more threatening than a spectre. As the days went by, my fears abated and I wondered if my experience had been a drunken hallucination. The moon had run almost a full cycle when, more through curiosity than fear, I took a stroll through the graveyard adjacent to the square.

In the far corner, hidden behind long grass, I

found it. A moss-covered stone, barely legible: "Thomas Rouse, 1637 – 1682, butcher, killed by wild beasts in this market."

What manner of creature could penetrate the city walls and haunt those dark passages? What wounds would lead the authorities to conclude that an animal was responsible? My forgotten fears resurfaced. Had Rouse had been a victim of the pale child? If so, how many others, too poor to afford a monument, had fallen prey to that vindictive ghoul?

I staggered back, and tripped over another stone half-hidden by weeds. I read the faint words: "William Drew, butcher, 1725 – 1750." Twenty-five years old, unlikely to have died naturally, even in those far-off days.

Trade was brisk that day, and my hopes of leaving early were dashed. The day had been overcast, but as the lamplighter began his work, the clouds departed to reveal a full moon. Anxiety enveloped me as I hurried to clear the stall and take what was left to the poorhouse. Around me the other traders had finished, and I found myself alone in the silent centre of the market.

A cold wind blew through the alleyways as I walked at pace towards the exit and the salvation of the city streets. I could hear carousing from the taverns, the noise of cartwheels on the cobbles, every sound a reminder that I was close to safety.

The child stepped out in front of me, a mere ten feet away. His eyes now glowed red, his body glowed with eldritch light, the hideous sharp nail aimed at my throat. The aroma of putrefaction assaulted my nostrils.

I dropped my bundle and sank to my knees, begging him for mercy, praying to the God I had forsaken. Still he came forward, his arm outstretched. Paralysed with fear, I was unable even to utter a cry for help from those in the unreachable streets beyond.

He was above me now, the foul miasma stronger than ever. I dared glance at his hand. The finger no longer pointed at my neck, but instead was directed over my head.

Somehow, I knew what I must do.

I turned and half-walked, half-crawled towards my stall, the awful spectre following me. With trembling hands I unlocked the cabinet under the counter and retrieved my strongest knife. I used it to pry up the rotting boards that lined the floor.

The child now pointed down at the cobbles I had exposed. I raked away the earth between them, and soon was able to pull out the heavy blocks. When I had done this, I scraped at the hard earth beneath.

Bones glistened in the moonlight. A small skull confirmed they belonged to a child. Watched by my persecutor, I gathered up the relics, placing them with as much dignity as I could muster into my bag. Together we walked to the graveyard where I used the knife to dig a hole in the shadow of the great church. There I buried the remains, mumbling a prayer as I did so.

When I had finished, I looked up.

The boy had vanished.

Since then I have succeeded my father, and my stall is the most profitable in the market. My sons help me now. Often, when the nights are clear and the moon bright, I find a gold sovereign in my takings that I do not remember receiving.

I have decided to put some of my new fortune towards a proper funeral for the murdered boy.

For on those same nights I sometimes catch a glimpse of a vague shimmering figure pointing towards the churchyard.

The pale child has not yet achieved the peace he craves.

THE COAT

by Bonnabelle Downing

Sorting through Mum's accumulation of unnecessary paraphernalia was the most frustrating thing I'd ever had to do. Out-dated clothes, tattered books, broken ornaments, tangles of wool, papers yellowed with age, all stuffed into plastic bags, battered cases and leather trunks. Why she had saved all this rubbish I would never know. They would have to be disposed of. Just like Mum's brain had decided to reduce her memories, as if it too couldn't cope with the clutter. The trouble was it had reduced the memories too much and Mum was slowly becoming a stranger, a frail, slightly irritable imposter that never smiled with her eyes like she used to. Now her brows seemed permanently knitted in to a frown, her lips pursed in a kind of irritable sulk.

'What are you doing with that? That's mine, leave it alone!' she snapped accusingly, her shrill voice cut through me. Feeling like a naughty child I dropped the tattered, old coat I was holding up.

'We talked about this Mum, you can't take everything. There won't be room.'

She stared at me defiantly, her once kind eyes narrowed 'I told you, I'm not going anywhere. And in any case I need that coat.'

I picked the overcoat up again and held it at arm's length. Faded burgundy velvet, though once it must have been stylish now it smelled of mothballs and mould.

'I had my first man in that,' she whispered, and all at once the frown was gone. Her face took on a girlish impishness, her mouth curved into a coy smile.

'Mum!' I gasped, embarrassed.

'What?' She was annoyed with me again. 'I was young once you know. I did 'have a life' as they say. And this coat, well, I haven't told you this before but that was the beginning of it.'

I sat down, my mouth open in amazement. For the first time since that awful diagnosis of dementia, the visit to the care home and the subsequent row about her living arrangements, Mum was talking to me properly, like there was nothing wrong with her at all. The doctor had told me there'd be lucid moments like this but still I was taken aback.

'We met on Norwich market, 1947. I was sixteen, he was older. A German. Prisoner-of-War.'

I was intrigued. Was this really true?

'Why was he here? How come there were Germans waking about? Weren't they sent home once the war finished?'

'Oh eventually, but they were allowed to live here and wander about for a few years. Lived in a camp near Sheringham and had hardly any money.

He probably couldn't afford to get back home. They'd hang about near the market. It was the centre of Norwich back then, the cheapest and liveliest place to buy absolutely anything. They had a hard time though, boys would shout silly bits of German at them out of little phrase books and old men would glare at them or sometimes spit. Of course, apart from young girls no one liked them being here that much. Them and the Italians. The Germans wore black jackets and trousers and looked so handsome while the Italians were in mud brown, not so sexy.' Her lips curled in to that impish smile again.

'Mum!'

'What? Oh Lucy, you're such a prude. Just like my friend Heather. "Oh Joyce", she'd say, "what are you thinking, going after a German? He'll only want you to 'do it' then he'll leave you high and dry." But I didn't care. I was wearing the coat you see and it gave me the power I'd never had.'

I looked at her quizzically and she sighed.

'You don't know what it was like back then. Everything was so valuable, nothing was thrown out. We were encouraged to 'make do and mend'. Not like nowadays. I'd had my old coat since I was twelve. Mother had made it herself with cheap material bought off the market. Every year she'd take it out a bit but by the time I was sixteen it was a breaking point. She had to stretch it tight across my chest and it flattened me completely. We couldn't afford a new one, she said. Then, one day I was on the market shopping with my Aunt Nelly and I saw this beautiful coat hanging up, the one in your hand. It was so gorgeous; I just couldn't stop staring at it.

"It's the New Look", the stall-holder told me. "All the rage in London, this style. Feel how soft them curled whorls of fur are on the collar and cuffs? That's called astrakhan, from new-born lambs. Can you believe that? Try it on!"

Well, she didn't have to ask twice. I yanked my old childish coat off before you could say 'knife' and it was the strangest feeling, like I knew there and then that I'd never put it back on. The moment I slipped that new coat on and felt the way it fitted so perfectly over my bust and how the bodice nipped me in at the waist I changed inside. It was like I'd grown two inches taller, like I was a flower-bud that'd opened, like a chrysalis turned in to a butterfly. The stall- holder was so over-come with emotion she got tears in her eyes and Aunt Nelly stood there gawping at me and even people passing by stopped to stare. I felt like a film-star. Like Rita Hayworth or Jane Russell. Aunt Nelly and me looked at my old coat and we both knew it'd be a crime for me to have to put it back on. The stall-holder was so impressed with how I looked in it she said she'd reduce the price and Aunt Nelly, bless her, she bought me the coat there and then even though it cost so many clothes coupons it probably meant she wouldn't be able to buy anything new for herself for a year!

And the next day there I was at the market again

only this time I had the coat on. I'd coloured my lips with beetroot juice and put boot polish on my eyelashes. My hair was thick and jet black and I'd curled it in rags the night before. I felt like suddenly I knew what my body was for. As if I was the best looking girl in the world and do you know, looking back, I probably was!

The market was really crowded; lots of young mothers with shiny prams, housewives in their worn-out clothes buying what they could afford with their coupons. Things on the market were so much cheaper than in the shops then. All the stallholders were crying their wares loudly. Stockings were in short supply so that stallholder was popular. "Come on girls," he'd got this risqué patter "I'll help you try them on if you like!" It was all a bit of a laugh. Then there was the sweet-seller with his tub of unwrapped sweets, picking them up and letting them fall through his bare hands with no regard for hygiene. No, there was no health and safety in those days. There were baby chicks for six pence each. They were sold as sort of toys for whining children, taken home only to die the next day. No one saw anything wrong in that. And at the back of the market were all the cheap stalls. There was always a sort of reverse auction going on at the back and it was interesting to see just how low the price would fall before someone actually bought something.

So that day, I stood there in the crowd, feeling ultra-modern and grown up in my amazing, warm coat and suddenly there he was next to me, this tall, blond, incredibly good-looking German. I remember his name to this day. I'll never forget it. Conrad Bestman. We caught each other's eye and when the auction finished he followed me round the market from stall to stall and it turned into a game with him hiding behind the fish stall, then me pretending not to be interested and swishing past him in the coat, looking anywhere but at him, then both of us standing side by side at the fruit and veg stall, picking up fruit, apples, plums, fondling them suggestively, not saying a word just little glances at each other now and then until he picked up a huge marrow and we both burst out laughing at the same time.

We walked round the market arm in arm then, pointing, laughing, pretending we were going to be married and buying stuff for the home; a beautiful, willow-pattern tea-set, cushions for the living room, wool for the baby I would hopefully be expecting, pots for the kitchen and material for the shirt I was going to make for my handsome new husband.

As the light faded the stalls started to pack up for the night. We climbed the steps up to City Hall and sat with our arms around each other like we'd known each other all our lives, like the war had meant nothing, his hand stroking the softness of my magic coat, over-looking the brightly coloured stripes of Norwich Market, the place that had so unexpectedly become my very own Eden.'

Mum reached out, pulled the coat to her and buried her face in the fabric. 'Oh dear, the smell of him is all gone. But I can still remember it so clearly in here.' She tapped her head. 'Later that evening, when the market was all boarded up, we went round the back and well, you can imagine what happened.'

'Mum!'

'Oh yes, I'll never forget it. My first time. Wonderful it was. Wunderbar! I kept my coat on though,' and she covered her face with her hands and peeped out through her fingers like an embarrassed teenager.

'After that we'd meet on the market every chance we could. He'd fallen in love with me of course. He even bought me a cheap ring off the jewellery stall.' Her eyes wandered around the room. 'He had to go back home a few months later but he wrote to me every month for years afterwards, even after I'd met and married your Dad. I've still got his letters and that ring somewhere about.'

All at once I realised; Mum's stuff that I had so thoughtlessly been about to throw out was not junk, not unnecessary rubbish at all. Each item contained a memory or brought back a feeling. Who knew what other stories would be lost if I discarded it? There had to be another way. I could cut down my hours at work, reduce my spending, get in some help if necessary.

I looked at Mum with new eyes. Before she was my Mother she was a girl, full of energy and excitement and hope for the future. And what did doctors know anyway? One test and they'd written Mum off like a malfunctioning computer. If I could spend some time bringing the girl she once was back to life it would all be worthwhile. Hadn't she cared for me when I was a troublesome girl? Now it was my time to repay the debt.

'Come on Mum.' I stood up. 'We're going out.'

Immediately her eyes filled with fear and mistrust 'Not the Home?'

'No, I said gently, taking the coat and laying it down carefully on the settee. 'You won't be going there again. I just thought we could take a trip to the market. Come on, let's see what we can find.'

THE NIGHT MARKET

by Peter Loftus

Adults never really listen to children. They say they do, and they pretend to, but they don't really. 'Shhh,' they say. They want us to be quiet and at peace so they can return to whatever it is adults use to fill their days with meaning.

I was nine when my nana took me to the night market. It was the only thing she could do. But listen to me. I am older now and should know enough to start a story at the beginning.

My parents took me out that morning, down the coast to where the waves washed azure against the grainy white stacks we called the Three Sisters. Gulls wheeled so slowly they appeared frozen in the sky. My mother spread a cloth, white lace that rippled in the breeze, before spreading baklava, meatballs, yogurt laced with curling mint leaves and dotted with raisins, and bowls of tabbouleh. She poured sherbet, tart and refreshing from a metal flask. For once, just for a fleeting hour, the years melted from her face. All of the things that had happened, all of those lonely nights she spent searching the night skies for an answer, an answer that never came, faded away.

It was as if for that one afternoon she set down the yoke. She straightened. The wind from the sea blew her hair back from her face and she became younger, as I had only ever seen her on the wedding photograph framed and hanging in our hallway. She was magnetic.

I saw my father lift a tendril of hair from her cheek and lean forward to kiss her.

I didn't know at the time what I was doing. I had tiptoed closer to the edge of the cliff, a broad anvil of sun-baked sandstone. The breeze stirred the hairs on my arms, cooling. I could taste salt from the spray. How could it reach so high? The rocks below reminded me of my dogs' teeth, darker at the roots, hungry. I don't remember any impulse – just my doll's face receding as she fell towards the water. Had I meant to drop her? I had no idea.

It wasn't until we were in the car and on the way back home that it hit me. My mother asked, 'What happened to your dolly?' It was as if I had just then noticed her absence and realised what I had done. Tears filled my eyes immediately. I was inconsolable. I cried all the way home as the sun set and the sky turned a dark blue. Towns and villages passed in strings of light along the shining windows of the car, the mountains in the distance a black cutout before the wheeling stars.

But I didn't see any of that. I sobbed and sobbed until my head ached and the snot dried on my cheeks. My mother shushed and stroked my ankles mile after mile until her hand grew still and her brow began to return to its familiar furrowed shape.

My father carried me back to the house wrapped in the lace blanket. I remember one hard crumb left over from the picnic pricking my thigh. He put me in the women's parlour and turned out the light. 'I will leave the door open,' he said.

My grandmother appeared and stroked my hair. She whispered in the darkness, kind words, I think, but I was deaf to them.

When I awoke the next morning, the net curtains were billowing and the room was lit like a lantern with bright morning sun. I was still crying. Had I cried all night or just started again when I awoke?

Faces came and went. My mother, bowed and tired once more. My father, proud but caring. My nanna with her eyes flat and dark, like stones in a river bed. She always looked at me like she could see straight into my thoughts and didn't like what she saw. The old witch was right. Later they dressed me, and fed me a little, but I knocked the bowl to the floor and ran back to my room. All I could see was the doll, my precious one, falling downwards and away from me, into the frothing waves.

And so it was that when the balmy darkness came and the cicadas started to sign, my grandmother came to take me to the night market.

'Pickle,' she cooed. 'We are going to the night

market. You can choose whatever you want. A new dolly. A mizmar. A pretty box to lock up your secrets and treasures. Whatever you want.' I did not answer and so she went on. 'And you can have food too. Zainab fingers dripping with honey.'

And then the car slowed and our driver opened the door. I must admit, I was curious and excited. For the first time in a day, my tears slowed.

A muezzin called the last call to prayer, a sound that was strangely dreamy. Jasmine filled the air, blood lily, cemetery iris. Spices too, rippled in waves through the dusk so that I imagined a scarf of orange, brown, gold passing beneath the awnings at the mouth of the souk. I smelled more; roasted goat, ladled in its own fat since sunrise made my mouth water and reminded my stomach how little I had eaten.

The narrow entrance led to a world of wonder. A thousand lamps glittered and glimmered, their dark wood carved with intricate designs of leaves, birds, leaping fish. Their latticed sides threw coloured patterns on the arched vault of the bazaar. Incense made my eyes itch, heady and rich. People moved to and fro, shadowy forms made gaudy by the parti-coloured light. Their passage down the stalls was like fish working their way down a reef. There were spices too, piled high in linen sacks – cinnamon, nutmeg, chilli, sumac. I wanted to plunge my hands into their cool depths and feel them scrunch between my fingers. A tall man turned to stare at me, his fingers stained yellow with spices. On the left, a caged monkey with the face of a boy bared its fangs to me.

The sound of chanting came from further back and the fluting call of pipes, a gentle but insistent drumming and plucked zither.

'What would you like?' My grandmother tugged at my arm, as if to propel me towards my desires.

I stared, open-mouthed. I have always hated making choices. Once you point your finger and say 'That one,' the world of possibilities collapses.

'Come on. Would you like something to eat? A new dolly?'

I picked at my lip.

Nana's eyes were wells of liquid darkness.

'Nothing?'

I shook my head.

'Maybe further in. Let's find out what is troubling you.' She was a shrewd woman.

We wove deeper into the maze. Lanterns, carpets, leather goods, trinket boxes, passed us by, a trove of treasures.

My eyes grew accustomed to the smoky incense. The aisle cooled as we walked, and we left the scent of food behind. Here smelled of dust and emptiness, like the rooms of a house no-one has lived in for years.

'I can help you,' called a man with kohl-eyes. A ruby serpent flared its hood and tested the air as we passed.

'No,' called my nana. 'Not you.'

An old lady rolled bone dice into an inlaid tray.

'Ah,' she said. 'The girl who cries. Please.' She gestured at the entrance to her stall. 'Come. I can find that which is lost.'

My nana shook her head. 'Not you. My thanks, though.'

We came at last to a wizened brown man hunkered outside a stall like a cricket on a leaf. His hands moved, passing a scorpion between. His stall held all manner of preserved creatures; beetles shining black against soft cotton, mice, red eyed and grinning in stoppered bottles of yellow fluid, strings of spiders, dried locust, staring lizards.

'You,' my grandmother called. 'Can you help me?'

The man turned away from her. 'No' mother. Not I.'

I felt a hand shove my back. 'Help this child. She has lost something and cries all night.'

The man finally looked at us, flashing gold teeth as he grimaced over his shoulder.

'No, mother. A thousand apologies. This is not the place for you.'

'I know of you, Hamad. I bought something from you years ago, when I was but a small girl.'

'I remember. And you know my price.' He looked at me then, his eyes full of sorrow. 'You cannot pay it.' The scorpion chose that moment to strike, plunging its stinger into the meat of his palm. His hand darted to his mouth. Tiny, yellow teeth crushed the scorpion's head before he swallowed it whole.

I tried to step back, but my nana had moved behind me and shoved me again.

'Since when did you forget how to speak? Lama, ask now. This man will help you, whether he wants to or not. It is his lot.'

Hamad shifted his moccasin-covered feet. There was no shifting of sand. I felt a wave of dizziness pass through my head. He was not touching the ground. The man was floating an inch of so above the packed dirt floor of the market. He tugged his ankles so that he sat there cross legged. 'Yes, my dear, you are right. Your eyes do not deceive you. My sort cannot profane themselves by touching the soil. Nor do we cast a shadow.'

My mouth was dry, my voice lost somewhere deep within.

'I know what you want.'

'No.' It was the first time I had spoken.

'That is not the question. You want that which you have lost.'

'Yes.'

'The question is what are you willing to pay?'

'She dropped her doll into the sea,' said my grandmother.

Hamad's wise brown eyes never left mine.

'Please. Can you bring back her doll?'

Hamad smiled, still not taking his eyes off mine. 'That's not what she wants and a small task for one with power such as mine.'

My nana coughed. 'A doll. That is all.'

The man reached behind him and plucked an empty jar from a low shelf. 'No. Not all.' He produced a bulging goat-skin and started to fill the jar with yellow liquid. ‘Well?’

‘I want my brother back. Saad, my little messenger, the boy who always made me smile.’

My grandmother hissed like a scalded snake and stepped back. ‘No. Lama! It is too great a thing to ask. The price...’

Hamad ignored her. ‘And what happened to this bringer of good news?’

‘She killed him. She slapped him in the street and he fell backwards, into the path of a lorry.’

My nana grasped the back of my hair, her hand a skeletal claw. ‘Foolish girl!’ She struck me in the side of the head. ‘Liar! He was rude and disrespectful, as are you. It is not my fault he fell. I was just doing my job, educating him.’

‘And what will you give me, my child?’ Hamad turned the jar softly in his hands as he spoke.

‘Her,’ I said lifting my head towards the crone behind me. ‘Gladly.’

There was a flash of blue light and the space filled with a dense white smoke. My ears hummed as if someone had just clapped their hands to either side.

The jar in Hamad’s hands now held a struggling rodent. Hamad pressed the lid shut and smiled. And then, at last and beyond all hope, my brother was walking towards me and taking my hand. He grinned up at me, showing the gap where his two front teeth had never grown in. ‘I’m hungry,’ he said. ‘Can we get something to eat?’

‘Of course we can,’ I said. ‘Whatever you like.’

TRADERS

by Mary Outram

There aren't many white faces at Kigali market so I wasn't surprised when this tall European homed in on me. He stepped into the space at my elbow and briefly I caught the scent of a musky aftershave. I was buying mangoes, he asked in English if I could choose some for him. I said, 'How many?'

He said 'four', but then he didn't have a bag, so we went over to the painted gourd stall and he found a bag with a stripe on it, a cotton bag. He asked if I'd like to go for a coffee. It was my lunch hour, I said, 'OK'.

We went out into the full sun, over the road and into Billy's cantina. We sat at a small wooden table, with sticky oilcloth mats. He said, 'I think I've seen you at the Swedish embassy. I remember your hair. It's unusual, blonde and wavy. Messy. I like it.'

I smiled. 'I'm a clerk. I don't think you are.'

He nodded and looked at his coffee. He said, 'Can you help me? Something besides buying fruit?'

'It depends what you want?'

'I'm looking for an old friend and maybe she'll

come to one of your parties at the embassy. She used to.'

'What's her name?'

'Anneke Bron.'

'Why don't you ask our office to trace her?'

He leant towards me and said, 'It's delicate. We were in love, but I was married so she didn't want to commit, we lost touch. Now I'm free. Maybe if she's on the guest list you could tell me in private? You could give me a ring?' He stood up to go. He reached into his back pocket, took out a leather wallet and said, 'I should give you something for the call.' I saw the edges of a lot of banknotes. Two were put on my side of the table, green American money – worth half my salary for the month. He gave me his card with his number and left. I picked up the cash and put it in my skirt pocket. I watched him walk away down the baked clay road, the strap of the bag over his shoulder.

I suddenly remembered we're always watched at work, but I don't know if we're tailed when we're outside. When I got back to the embassy I put on my jacket - the air conditioning is Arctic so we can wear suits - then went to see the Security Chief, Pitor. He's thick necked and wears open collars. He took the man's card and read out the name: 'Arkardi Lenov, Russian Embassy, Rwanda. Did he give you money?' I put one of the notes on the desk in between us. Pitor laughed, he said, 'OK. Here's what we do: you look out for the woman's name in the guest lists and let me know if you see it.' He picked up the note and the card, put them in the mouth of a red stapler and snapped the two together. Did he know about the other note? When I got home I put it in a book. It had meant nothing to Lenov - just a tip, a pleasantry, but now I felt uncertain about having it.

A day later Pitor called me in to see him but kept me waiting while he signed some papers. He likes using paper – it sidesteps Internet hackers. Behind him on the wall was a painting of a yacht in full sail, and to one side, through a door, I could see a bank of live CCTV screens. Did they film at the cafe? Could I be sure he didn't know about the money? Pitor put down his pen, he said, 'Our friend has a minor post at the Russian embassy in agricultural science. Any news of the woman?

I said, 'No.' Then I swayed from foot to foot, keen to get away before he could decide to mention the cash. Pitor waved his hand. I had to get back to work anyway; I was organizing an event, a fund-raiser, for the ambassador's charity that helps rural schools.

The next day there was a kerfuffle in Europe. Some Russian diplomats were kicked out of France. There was the usual photo in the newspapers of a diplomat putting a large cardboard box into a car.

I went to the market early on Saturday. I was buying dried beans from an open sack when Lenov appeared. He stood very near; I didn't mind. I said, 'More mangoes?'

He said, 'No. But thank you. A quick coffee?'

I said, 'OK. But how did you know I'd be here?'

He said, 'I took a gamble – I thought you looked like a morning person.'

I said, 'You were right.'

We sat at a different table in Billy's - one further into a corner. Lenov had an espresso in a peach coloured cup. He said, 'I'm leaving the country very soon. I'm packing up, I found this bag; I thought you might like it?' The bag he'd bought at the market had been folded into a square. He passed it across the table.

I said, 'There's no news of your friend. I'm sorry.'

He nodded, got up and left. I assumed he'd been redeployed. I finished my coffee and walked home for lunch.

In the afternoon I had a French lesson with Madame Ngatu and in the evening my dance class. I want to improve my CV. Rwanda is a "stepping stone" appointment for ambassadors; I need to be ready to move too. On Sunday I read the papers – all about the wars, the looting, the talks.

On Monday morning I went to report the bag to Pitor but he was unavailable, stuck in meetings. The alternative was his deputy - a prat who'd left his laptop in a taxi in Copenhagen and the Danes love it when Swedes make a mistake. I put the thing away. I did log it, there's a ledger for gifts received at work; clerks get given stuff like illustrated copies of the Bible and plastic snorkel sets.

At the end of the week I decided I'd have a treat - a water melon. I'd seen a pyramid of them in the side markets near hands of green bananas. I would need an extra bag; I got out Lenov's. When I shook it open, a square blue envelope fell out, 'Anneke' was written on the front. Pitor would have to know.

It was nearly five o'clock, but to get it over with I went to his office. His PA said he was in the function room in the ambassador's residence - the other side of the building. It's a hike to get over there and I got held up by the tea-trolley coming the other way. The function room is a double height room with a dais at one end for the Swedish flag. Pitor and our technician were talking by a display cabinet. The ambassador collects statuettes, mainly standing figures. Some are antiques, some copies - they live in the cabinet, a little plenary crowd behind glass doors - conversation pieces. My favourite's a fake, a ten inch alabaster Assyrian with his hands clasped at heart level. I handed over the envelope and rushed off.

I should have refused that money when Lenov got out his wallet. I couldn't spend it; I couldn't put it in the bank. It could look like a bribe. The odds Pitor knew were fifty-fifty. If I'd been seen, I needed a way out.

After two weeks not Anneke Bron, but another "A Bron" - Dr Arnos Bron, showed up on the office computer. A team leader with the UN weapons inspectorate, previously in Iraq. He was invited to evening drinks with the ambassador, plus his unit. I went along the corridor to tell Pitor, he nodded, reached for a hefty manilla file on his desk and I got out of the room, but not before I read Lenov's name on the folder and glimpsed another square blue envelope, this time with a Swedish stamp. Not many people send us letters from home. We don't deal with passports or visas here; the old colonial power, the Belgians, they do that for us up the road. Could it be from Lenov? Why was the file so big? The odds that I'd been observed at the café had just gone up.

Our staff numbers are lean and I was put on reception duty for the drinks party. I sat at an antique desk and greeted people once they came through security. It was an all male group of twelve; multilingual chat, two in linen suits, some in shirt sleeves and several wore those waistcoats with lots of pockets, Bron included. They signed in. Bron was tall and bulky. Everyone was guided to the function room and I was told to stand down. I went to my cubicle and did admin until I was buzzed to get ready to sign everybody out.

I'd just reached the desk when I saw Pitor trotting through the main door with a guard behind him. The men from the reception were beginning to meander down to me; they were chatting with each other and one was still eating cake. When they were all out of the door I got up to leave, but Pitor came back inside with Bron and one of the weapons inspectors, a small guy in a suit, who was being gripped at the armpit by the guard. They hustled past and I didn't know whether to put them in the book or not, so I made notes on a separate piece of paper and waited.

An attaché I recognized from the Russian embassy arrived. He was wearing a Manchester United shirt. He was flushed, not quite steady on his feet. The phone on the desk rang; I was to bring the attaché to the conference room. When we got there Pitor was sitting with Bron, the small man, the ambassador and her aide. Two armed guards were by the door. I mouthed the word "Coffee?" at Pitor and he shook his head. On the table was a figure from the ambassador's collection – a terracotta girl, palm-sized and ancient, a gift from the Egyptians.

I went back to the foyer. Soon afterwards Bron and the aide left the building; the aide was carrying a briefcase. I sat and waited. The two security men on the door tried to make me laugh by doing ballroom dancing round the lobby, until one of them touched his finger to his plastic earpiece. Bron and the aide came back inside - they went straight past me. The phone on the desk rang - now Pitor wanted coffee. When I took the tray into the conference room there were two more statuettes on the table. They were similar to the Assyrian one that I like, but dusty.

I returned to the foyer. Fifteen minutes later Bron walked past me, head up. Ten minutes after that the Russian attaché left, together with the little man, whose name I'd worked out from the invitation list was Mekelev. The attaché went ahead, fists clenched. Mekelev turned his face to me, he was pale, he blew a kiss then he was gone. The phone rang, I was told to go home.

Next day I took Pitor the register and my notes. He opened his desk drawer, took out Lenov's calling card and the banknote. He unpicked the staple with a knife, put the dollars in front of him and looked up at me.

I said, 'I think that should go to charity. In fact, I'd like to double it.'

Pitor laughed, he said, 'That's my girl. Don't talk about this, but Mr Lenov traded a thieving school friend for a job at Uppsala University. Good luck to him.'

Pitor waved his hand and I left - I didn't hurry away.

THE TRANS SAHARA HIGHWAY

by Claire Wood

There was something about the way the sun beat down that day. The way the dust flicked up and formed a layer on his flip-flops and between his toes. The way the dappled light through the striped canopy landed on the stall in front of him. The way people kept to the shade to avoid the intensity of the heat.

A memory flickered far back of his head. What was that? He'd last encountered that smell in a sister market over six thousand miles away. The charred, acrid smell of spit-roasted pork, spiked by spices not normally found here.

Six thousand, six hundred and ninety-four miles away in fact. One hundred and fifty-one hours by road on the Trans Sahara Highway, through Algeria, Niger, Chad... He'd once googled it when he was missing it the most. A sign caught his eye. NEW – KENYAN BARBEQUE. So, a little bit of his homeland had also made it north to Norwich.

He closed his eyes and stood stock still. He let people move past him while he allowed the memory to grow. His mind could traverse six thousand miles if he let it.

Suddenly he was a small boy again holding someone's hand. Safe. Secure. Soft.

His mother smiling and telling him he could ask for the bananas today and pay for them himself.

'Ndizi kumi tafadhali.'

The feeling of pride when he'd successfully completed the transaction. The wide stallholder's smile, generously slipping him a passion fruit as his reward for being so grown up. How old had he been then? Three maybe four? Proudly carrying the ten bananas home. The echoing cries from the older boys selling street melons. And the sharp smoky smell of the barbequed meat, slow roasted over a fire a few stalls further. His mother's soft hand. His sister swaddled on her back. The sandy paths. The dust between his toes.

They say grief can be drawn. Draw a circle and write 'life' in the middle. That is your life when it first happens. When it first happens, grief takes over your whole circle. Your whole life.

But in time, life grows around the grief like a vine in full sun. It never goes away but your life around it fills with other things. Some important. Others not so. But it still fills. The circle grows smaller as your life grows around it.

It's true. His life had grown around his grief. He had his football and the joy of being grabbed by his friends when they scored. The delicious moment when a friend flashed him a smile. The shared victories. He'd learnt to stockpile those moments, even though he was still a teenager, unsure of himself. Unsure even how old he was. Not able to answer the question all kids are asked. Sixteen? Maybe seventeen? There was no one to ask.

But slowly he'd started to make a life for himself here in Norwich. He longed for fulltime, fulfilling work but that was still a long way off. Roshan at the charity was going with him next week to hand over his asylum application. Two trains and a bus to get to some office in Liverpool, just to hand it over in person. It was a joke. And then. Even then, they had no way of knowing if his case would be successful.

But he was almost certain he would be granted asylum. Who could read his story and force him to return? In fact, it was the high probability that he would never return that hurt the most. It still made him catch his breath sometimes if he allowed his mind to wander. Panic would course through his veins and he'd have to breathe deeply until it passed. Never to visit his mother's grave or his brothers' and sisters' graves. Never to stand at the foot of Mount Kenya under the African plain trees. Never to hand over shilling to pay for bananas. Never to stand in a country it would take a week of driving non- stop, 24/7, to reach, if he took the

Trans Sahara Highway.

No. The loaded trucks with refugees were constantly streaming north, week after week, month after month, year after year. It would be a long time before anyone set off south to Embu. A long time before he ever set south.

He opened his eyes and inhaled the smell of the Kenyan spit-roasted pork. Maybe the Kenyan would need someone to help him run his stall and would know of stories of places he could barely recall. Maybe today he was standing at a crossroads. Take one path instead of another.

He walked tall between the stalls on the hill.

MEMBERS CHALLENGE SHIELD WINNERS

ADJUDICATORS COMMENTS

Lynsey White

A genuine well done to everyone who entered. Submitting anything of yours for judgement is a brave thing to do and an achievement in itself. If you have not been placed in my list on this occasion, I empathise having been in your shoes many time.

This is the writing life, you win some and you lose some. Sometimes we lose because the story didn't resonate with the particular tastes and foibles of the person judging them. Because a story isn't a jigsaw puzzle or a maths question in an exam, it is personal and complicated.

For me this is by no means an easy decision so you may take comfort from that. Another judge may have chosen other stories. I didn't just read them once. Beyond my first impressions important in itself of course, I wanted to see which stories would stick in my mind, which is also a very important thing.

So I read them over two weekends, letting them brood for a week in between.

A story worth its salt stays with you for a while, and it is fair to say that all my winning and commended stories are of this quality. So for the two weekends in September you took me on so many different journeys.

I went to the London Stock Exchange in war time and back in time to Victorian England, which is my favourite historical period, so well done to those writers who did that. I met some extraordinary characters, a mischevious Norwich Terrier, a putrified moonlit child with a hideous clawed finger, an auburn haired temptress beckoning a humble stall holder to climb a ghostly gallows one winter afternoon.

We had plenty of death on the market, in fact we had the market as a metaphor for death.

We had stabbings and heart attacks.

We entered a shadowy Kafkaesque Norwich, complete with a silent 'K', which seemed somehow appropriate in which sinister men were pulling the city's strings in a hidden building.

We had the meat market of the online dating world, which became a more literal type of meat market in the story's grisly finale. But it was this one in my opinion made the cleverest use of the market theme

Charles Dickens made not one, but two, appearances and elsewhere he gave a distinctive Victorian flavour to a heart warming present day tale of a homeless lad who finds a new family in time for Christmas. I visited Newgate Gaol by candlelight in 1849 and glimpsed Prince Albert on horseback. Across the stories I found wonderful names such as Penny Dreadful, Evo Doggit and Ned the Cockmaster.

I warmed to the tale of a poor cook unexpectedly made pregnant by a passing tradesman from a country market who bungled the baking of a strawberry tart to be served to Charles Dickens no less hence creating a new concoction, the Bakewell Pudding. While she whisked her frothing hen's eggs, I felt I was watching Victorian Week on the Great British Bakeoff. It was a kitchen and a world I could have spent much longer in.

But although every story I read had many things to commend it, equally it had to be said that all the stories, even my winning entries, had some degree of room for improvement. Speaking personally, everything I have published, or ever published, has room for improvement.

The thing is that short story writing is tricky. We get better at it the more we try but it never stops being difficult. And why should it? What good is a half-hearted story? Whether we literally tell a story aloud or tell it by writing it down, telling stories is a performance art.

Like the plate spinner in a circus, the writer needs all their powers of observation and concentration, a key eye for detail and a delicate touch, every time they open their mouths or lift their pens to begin a new story. Many plates must be spun at once and as soon as the story performance starts, we must spin all of the plates all of time, or else learn clever techniques as some of the grand stylists do to distract the eye from the things we are less good at. These plates have to do big important things that we can't avoid tackling whenever we write fiction, such as character, plot, voice, tone and structure.
Most of the stories I read spun particular plates more successfully than others. For instance, a confident voice or convincing sense of period detail didn't always go hand in hand with the spinning plates of character development or control of plot.

In the case of this competition there was still a predetermined plate called theme and the question of theme played a negligible role in my decisions, as story always comes before theme. I believe it is the writers' job to explore what things mean, and we ought therefore to be interested in responding with depth and integrity when responding to any given theme. So on a couple of occasions when it felt that it was merely a tick box exercise for the writer, I was very mildly disappointed.

Many stories chose first person narrators and this

was a particular plate that sometimes failed to spin. The voice of the story is always the voice of the person telling the story and sometimes I wasn't sure who that was.

In a couple of cases I didn't know the most basic things about the narrator and that may be something for the writers to take on board in future. Even peripheral first person narrators have to be fully realised and have to earn their place in the story because a short story can't afford to carry dead weight.

In the terms of the spinning plate we call structure I was looking for the stories that spoke to the writer Flannery O'Connor's observation that 'stories may be short, but they shouldn't be slight'. Some of the really well written stories I read were longing to be something else, anecdotes, character sketches or even novels.

One story I described in my critique as being like a train rattling past, so many intriguing things at the brightly lit windows, but never a chance to sit still and properly look at any of them.

A few stories did a bit too much telling instead of showing. That is not to say telling is not desirable but sometimes there was exposition, back story or explanation placed too flatly on the page. Whenever you stop the story action to tell the reader a necessary fact, be aware that you are waking them up from the fictive dream of the story, as novelist John

Gardner described it. There are always subtle ways of drip feeding, rather than spoon feeding exposition to the reader, usually behind the smoke screen of dramatic conflict.

There was some lovely writing here. You spooked me and you shocked me and you made me nod in recognition. I will certainly never look at Norwich market the same way again.

Ultimately the stories I chose as my winners were the ones that worked best to me as stories. They didn't want to secretly be something longer and they knew that primarily stories convince through the senses, and the reader needs something to see and hear and taste and smell and touch because that is how human's experience and understand the world whether the physical one that we all live in, or the dreamt up worlds that we visit temporarily through the magic of story. These stories, however they did it, stopped me, sat me down and showed me something.

My first prize winner did all these things and more. I like voices that announce themselves straight away and from all the stories I read, this had for me the surest sense of voice and pace and a lovely poetic density to some of its sentences. My first prize winner was also the one which took the biggest risk. If I am honest I think the openness of its ending will divide the crowd but every story I have ever won a prize for has divided the crowd. I think writing, like all true art, is about taking risk and I hope you will enjoy listening to my first prize winner as much as I enjoyed reading it.

1st Place

THE MARKET

by Phillip Vine

It had taken her half a dozen years to shift just one position and now Margaret had moved six places nearer the centre of the City Market since the change from spring to autumn.

'What's it all about, Joe?'

Her partner stuck the sharp end of a pencil in his left ear and smiled.

'I'm not surprised you're so damn deaf.'

A frown clouded Margaret's face. It was not her partner's most endearing habit, this excavation of wax from his ears, but the man's ready smile was some compensation.

'What are you worried about, Mags?'

'Six deaths in six months, what's that all about then?'

'So what if it gets you nearer the action?'

'You're the detective,' she said, 'you should be concerned about these things.'

'I'm only interested when people pay me to be interested.'

It was a conversation stopper and Margaret returned to her book about a man whose passion was poisoning.

'You don't think, do you?'

She pointed to the lurid cover of her paperback.

'Not in real life, love, no.'

Sometimes, Margaret was left breathless by the way her man could read her mind.

She had known him less than a year and yet here they were living together like an old married couple, reading each other's books and thoughts, completing each other's sentences, sharing each other's opinions on the latest public outrage and the government's inability to stem the incoming tide of xenophobia and violence in Knorwich and beyond the borders.

'How long have we..?'

'Since last April, love,' Joe said.

It was how the City Market worked, this promotion through expiration.

When Margaret had inherited the stall that sold second hand books from her sister, she also received the numerical marker that had to be displayed at all times during the market's opening hours of eight until late, except on Sundays.

She had started out at Stall Number Twelve and now she was Stall Number Six. Yesterday she had moved within the inner circle of pitches that surrounded Karen Marshall's Stall Number One, from which the former teacher with the fat gold ear rings sold healing herbs and other magical concoctions of her own secretive devising.

Today was Wednesday and, by the close of a sunlit Thursday evening, both Karen Marshall and her niece, Shelley Noble, were dead.

On Friday morning, Margaret was presented with the deeds to Stall Number Four by the Mayor of Knorwich.

'What was it this time?'

Joe's voice was relaxed, affable, Saturday evening mellow with Sunday best still to come.

'It's not a game, Joe.'

Margaret was sweating and irritable and slightly afraid.

'Well, when you're in my line of business, Mags, you've seen it all.'

'It was a knife, actually.'

'Was it, my word?'

'The same knife, wielded by the same man, the same madman from across the Yare, that did for them both, an outlander, known to the police, they said.'

'Was it, indeed?'

Margaret slammed the door to the living room, stormed upstairs and turned on the shower.

As the healing heat of the water cleansed her from her sins of fear and anger, she thought of Joe, and how little she really knew him.

'Where did he come from, just like that, just like a miracle?'

Her words were caught by the downward strikes of the hot water and washed away with her worries about the murders at the market.

Even so, she half expected Joe to answer her question, to hear his words rising like steam up the spiral staircase of their home.

'I came from two rivers hence, I came because you called me, to rescue you from the pains of loneliness.'

That's what he would have said, Margaret thought, never giving her the information she really needed, really wanted.

'Damn cheek,' she said, almost choking on the burning water and suds of soap, 'I never needed rescuing.'

'I came in response to your advertisement in the Knorwich Crier.'

'Yes,' Margaret said, 'that's exactly what he did say when we first met.'

Minutes later, she was dressing in her Saturday night clothes.

Joe liked her to look the part when they made love.

On the Monday morning, the police were buzzing about City Market like flies, stinging like wasps.

Questions, questions, questions.

'What's going on?' Margaret said to Jess Arber who was Stallholder Number Three and sold a nice line in tacky frames reputed to have once enclosed great works of art.

'Don't know, don't care.'

'They've got him already, haven't they?'

'We're both nearer now to the centre of the market, aren't we?'

Margaret watched the red backs of Jess's hands as she dealt the frames to potential customers.

'This one here,' her friend said, 'this gold one used to hang in the Classics Room in Knorwich Castle.'

'Really?'

'Yes, it held a Rubens in its gilded arms.'

Margaret smiled at the expertise, the patter.

'I don't know,' Jess said, 'which are more stupid, the police or the tourists.'

Margaret had known her for all of the six years she had worked in the City Market.

Death by recent death, they had both moved closer to the hub of the market's wheel of stalls.

'Aren't you afraid, Jess?'

The police were gone, the tourists were in abatement, and Margaret's voice was cold as stone.

The rest of the week at the market passed without major incident. Margaret was busy with her books, gratified by the increased trade now that she had progressed nearer to the beating heart, the soul of Knorwich Market. She was especially pleased at the trading of a first edition of an Eric Brown, picked up in the Oxfam shop in Magdalene Street for coppers, now sold for thousands to a tourist who had only paused to ask the way to the cathedral.

'Which one, love?'

The woman fingered the rosary about her neck.

'Up the hill, that's the Catholic one.'

The woman made no immediate move, continued counting her beads, her lips moving in rhythm with her silent prayers.

'I've got a nice Eric Brown here,' Margaret said, 'if you're interested, that is.'

On the Saturday evening, however, just as Joe had turned the last page of Reginald Hill's final Dalziel and Pascoe, just as he was about to recommend the novel to Margaret, the telephone in the hall became too insistent to ignore.

'It's always for you,' he said.

For one moment, Margaret paused to consider why a successful private detective never received calls at home.

'It's because I like to keep the work at work, Mags.'

Joe's voice was calm and logical as always and she dismissed the questions that flew about her head like fighting birds.

'It's Jess's Dick,' she whispered, 'he says she's dead.'

The telephone fell from her hands and broke apart upon the unforgiving floor.

'Can't you do something, Joe?'

'Well,' he said, 'we could consider the evidence?'

'No, I meant haven't you got any connections?'

'I never worked with the Officials, Mags, I never worked in Knorwich.'

'What do you do now, then?'

She thought of how Joe always left for his office after she had left for the City Market, of how he was always back in her house before she returned, how she had never seen his place of work.

'I mean,' he said, 'not until I moved in with you.'

She thought, too, of the food and flowers always on the table when she arrived home, and now felt guilty for her earlier thoughts.

'Well, look, Mags, I've done some work with the City Fathers, so I'll see what I can do, see what I can find out for you.'

'Look, I'm Stallholder Number Three, and I'm scared to death.'

'You never told me, Mags, you never said what Kathy died of.'

'Don't you know?' she said. 'You know everything.'

Her voice was bitter as wormwood.

Ten days later, on a Wednesday morning heavy with grey frost, Margaret was negotiating a price for a rare anniversary reissue of Phillip Vine's vampire novel, when she heard the dull click of what might have been the cocking of a pistol.

She half turned her head but her customer was insistent.

'It's got sticker shadows front and back and it's got foxing and it's got red biro scribbles on page thirty two and it might even be an ex-library copy.'

The woman's face was blotched with cold and spleen.

Or it might just have been the click of a roulette ball from May Townshend's casino in the next door pitch.

'And it's a shit novel anyway.'

Margaret knew the customer was always right was the iron rule of the City Market, but unwarranted comments on the quality of a book she had loved since her teenage years was too much.

'Fuck off,' she said, and watched with horror as her spittle landed – at the same time as her words – on the woman's lined and patched face.

Margaret's anger, and subsequent apology, meant she missed the gunning down of May Townshend as she spun her final wheel of fortune.

'It's red,' someone shouted. 'I've won, it's number three.'

That night, Margaret downed an entire bottle of shery and, in the morning, called in sick.

'You're never sick,' the City Market manager told her.

'I'm frightened,' she said.

'You'll lose your pitch.'

'Good,' she said, and turned off her mobile phone.

'You don't mean it,' said Joe.

'I do.'

'Look,' Joe said, 'one thing I've learned over the years is that you can run, you can hide, but, if your number's up, they'll always find you.'

It was the most chilling thing her man had ever told her but she knew it was true.

'Are you going out, Joe?'

He was placing his private dick's trilby hat upon his head.

'Yeah, Mags, I'm off to City Hall to see what's going on.'

She followed him out of the door.

'Glad to see you thought better of it, Margaret.'

The City Market manager's voice was dark and burbled like an underground stream.

'You're Stallholder Number One now.'

'Why? What's happened to Sally?'

'Heart attack.'

'What?'

'In the night, her husband called, woke me at five this morning.'

'I'm leaving, right now.'

'You can't do that, Margaret, you're Stallholder Number One.'

Margaret raised her head to see City police officials surrounding her pitch.

'How's your head now, Margaret?'

The City Market manager's voice was lighter, as if its babbling waters had found a point of stillness in a deep pool.

She began to lay out her books.

One of the officials picked up a battered hardback copy of Shirley Jackson's The Lottery, turned it over in his gloved hands.

'You a collector?'

Margaret's words were chipped from the ice in her soul.

'The wife is.'

She looked at the man's shiny navy blue uniform with its polished silver buttons.

'Can you help me?' Margaret said.

As the sun set that evening over the many coloured stalls of Knorwich City Market, Margaret Hatherwood folded away her unsold books.

There was a pride in her packing.

She had made it to the centre of the universe, to the hub of the market, and her profits on the day's trading had exceeded those for the rest of the year put together.

There was prestige and status and future profit in items purchased from Stall Number One.

Her dead sister, Margaret thought, would be proud of her.

On her way out, she handed a copy of The Lottery to the policeman with the shiny uniform.

'What's your wife's name?'

'Margaret,' he said.

'That's nice,' she said.

Joe was there as usual when she got home, flowers and food on the dining room table as always.

'Good day?' he said.

'Yes.'

'I wanted to do something special tonight, Mags.'

'Thank you,' she said, and her voice suddenly sounded shrunken, hollow as a hungry ghost's.

'I'm sorry, Mags, but I can't help you.'

Joe's voice was as kind as possible, given the circumstances.

'I know,' she said.

2nd Place

SWIPE LEFT

by Kathy Joy

Jazz music crooned in the background, each piano key a soft caress in my ears, accompanied by the low hum of conversation and the gentle clink of cutlery. I slid my phone across the table and peered at it. No missed calls or texts. No emails. No private messages. I studied the empty seat before me, hoping I wouldn't be stood up.

Smartly dressed waiters travelled between tables like bees courting flowers, hovering in before sweeping away. I lifted the wine glass to my lips and slowly sipped the dark fragrant liquid. Like the jazz, it was smooth and left a pleasant taste behind.

In an attempt to set my nerves at ease, I placed my handbag in my lap, checking the contents, ensuring I had everything I needed. Satisfied I was suitably equipped, I tucked it back under the table. Then, for the third time that evening, I picked up the wine list and scanned the various vintages, avoiding eye contact with the waiters and other diners.

My sister was the one who pushed me back into the dating world.

'You're never too old to put yourself on the market,' Julie told me one day over coffee.

At the time, I detested the phrase – like I was some prized pig to be poked, prodded and valued. The analogy was sadly accurate. Strangers would ogle my picture, measure me up, and decide if I was worth their time. Hypocritical as it was, I did the same as I perused each profile, looking for just the right swine to put a ribbon on.

'Dating is so much easier these days. You can do it all online,' Julie had continued.

I, meanwhile, remained silent. The idea of dating made me shudder. Better to be alone than be hurt again.

Julie set her hand on mine, her expression softening. 'Don't let that bastard take away your chance of being loved again.' Her lips curled into a loose smile. 'The only way you're going to get over this is to get back out there.'

At first, I resisted. I know my sister meant well, but she had no idea what it was like, couldn't possibly understand my fear. As time went by, though, I realised something had to change, and I relented. Julie excitedly showed me E-Harmony, Match.com, and various other dating sites. Then we covered the apps. The whole thing was confusing and took time to get used to, but I soon began to see the benefits of online dating.

I looked up and saw a man stroll into the restaurant. He looked just like his profile picture, right down to the slate grey suit. The only difference was that his photo didn't do justice to his steel-blue eyes.

He stopped, holding his phone out, looking between it and the sea of heads at their tables before he met my gaze. I waved. Those long legs ate up the burgundy carpet as he zeroed in on me.

'Shannon...?' He asked.

I nodded. 'You must be Isaac.'

His broad shoulders sank in relief, and he held out his hand. I grasped it, my mauve nail polish standing bright against the tan of his skin. Finally, he took his place opposite me.

'Sorry for being late. I couldn't find a parking spot.' His sheepish grin revealed teeth as white as glaciers.

'I wasn't waiting long,' I lied.

After a brief, awkward silence we began to chat. Isaac confided that he'd had a slow day at his law firm. I responded that Fridays always dragged, especially for a teacher. Working with five-year-olds is no easy feat.

We picked up our menus, perusing the cream pages with sharp black text listing various dishes, occasionally chancing mildly flirtatious glances at each other. We continued our conversation, keeping to safe topics like what we were ordering, what we thought of the restaurant and the perils of online dating.

Once the waiter took our order and scuttled

away, we began to wade deeper into the 'getting to know you' portion of the evening. So far I had learned that Isaac had a cat called Delilah, a penchant for rock climbing, and a weakness for Tom Clancy novels. He seemed nice. Then again, they always did. At first.

I remember meeting Jack at a pub in London. I was out with friends, but after Jack and I started talking, I left with him to get a bite to eat. At the restaurant, he was charming, all smiles. He even pulled my chair out for me. There was no way I could have known how much he'd hurt me. But this was not then. I knew so much more than I did five years ago.

'How long have you been a teacher?' Isaac prompted.

'About six years now.'

Isaac's eyes lit up, impressed. 'Do you enjoy working with children?'

'Very much. They can be a handful, but I love seeing their little smiles.' I took a quick sip of wine and tucked a strand of blonde hair behind my ear.

When our food was brought out, the conversation slowed, but it didn't stop. A light tingling travelled to my centre, jumping about in my stomach. Isaac was precisely the kind of man I'd been looking for.

The first course went down well, and we moved onto the second. All too soon we were devouring our dessert. Isaac got bolder and bolder, first touching my fingertips, then my hand.

Jack did that too. He was so confident, his laugh

infectious. A few drinks later and he invited me to his home. I wasn't foolish. I had been careful all night, watching my glass like a hawk, but he didn't slip anything in it. In fact, he'd been nothing but gentlemanly the entire evening. Before I left with him, I texted my girlfriends, letting them know where I was going and with whom. I wasn't drunk either – a little tipsy but perfectly aware of everything around me.

When it was time for the bill, Isaac insisted on paying. He had asked me out and picked the restaurant, he reasoned, so I graciously accepted.

As we walked out, side-by-side, we stole glances at each other. Neither of us wanted the date to end just yet so Isaac suggested we go to his place for drinks. Doubts began to surface, bringing with them unwelcome memories, but I quickly pushed them aside. I had to do this.

When we arrived at Isaac's flat, he poured two glasses of champagne, and we talked a little more. Talking became light, flirtatious kissing, and then Isaac stood and gestured for me to follow him.

'Let's take this to the bedroom,' he husked.

Isaac led me down the hall. I knew what was coming. My heart began to beat faster and faster. I wanted this – needed it. I reached into my bag, fingers searching for the protection I had brought for the occasion. When he opened the door at the end and allowed me into the dark room, I took it out, ready.

The door clicked closed. I inched in little by little, footsteps echoing. Then Isaac flicked the light on. It wasn't his bedroom.

There were bloodstained manacles on the wall, a wooden table stood to the side with knives, whips, and a set of scalpels lined along its surface. Plastic covered the walls and floor to make clean up easier. I gripped the handle of my protection tighter.

In the brief few seconds I had to take in the room, I heard Isaac come up behind me. I knew what he was going to do, could smell the chemicals he had doused the rag in his hand with.

Thoughts of Jack flashed through my mind – how he had pinned me to the floor of his living room and violated my body with his. After the disgusting deed was done, he rasped in my ear:

'I didn't make you come here – you chose to. You wanted it.'

I spun seconds before Isaac reached me, the silver of the knife blade glittering as I plunged it into his chest, hitting the heart dead on. All that practice had paid off.

Isaac gasped. He hadn't expected it. None of the men before him had either.

He sputtered like a waterlogged engine before collapsing. I yanked the knife out, watching the blood pool beneath his body. Those blue eyes looked almost grey as death took him.

Jack was caught and sent to prison. Most women don't get that luxury. Many don't even see their tormentors in court. I should have felt closure or at least relief, but I didn't. Perhaps it was because he was sentenced to just five years – five years was nothing compared to all he had taken from me. What happened that night was like a stain I couldn't clear. Sometimes I swore I could smell his rancid sweat and musky cologne on my skin no matter how much I scrubbed. I was afraid to leave my home. When I did go out, I saw him everywhere – that wolfish grin, and those wild eyes filled with lust and hatred.

It took me a while to realise that I was seeing him – not in person but that malignance inside him. The attack had left me able to recognise the predators amidst the smiling faces of the crowd. They stood out like blazing beacons as I flicked through the various dating profiles, or sat across the table from them in coffee shops and restaurants.

Tired of being scared, of being the helpless victim, I knew I had to fight back somehow. So I scoured dating sites looking for people like Jack. That's how I found Isaac. He'd called himself other names before. John. Paul. Joshua. All biblical names. I couldn't even begin to uncover his twisted logic as he lured women to his dungeon so he could violate them and then carve them like a Christmas ham. I may not have been Isaac's first, but I made sure I was the last.

Julie had been right. Putting myself back on the market was helping me.

Taking care not to tread in the blood, I stepped over Isaac's body, put on the rubber gloves I had brought with me and padded through his home, fishing through drawers and cupboards until I found what I was looking for. Like me, Isaac was careful. He had disposed of the evidence, but that warped mind of his couldn't help but keep souvenirs. Opening a shoebox beneath his bed revealed Polaroid photos of each of his victims chained to the wall in that room, lifeless. I tipped the pictures onto the dining room table, organising them into a macabre parade. When his body was found, everyone would know what kind of man he really was.

On my way to the front door, I made sure to take the wine glass I had drunk from. I couldn't leave any trace of myself behind. Outside, the winter air raised gooseflesh across my bare arms. I wanted nothing more than to retreat home and settle under a duvet, maybe enjoy a well-deserved tub of Ben and Jerry's, but there were still things to be done.

It took me a few hours to wipe all the evidence clean and spread the knife, the champagne glass, and my blonde wig across the city. I changed clothes in a public toilet and burned my evening dress in an isolated park, leaving nothing but ash.

Garbed in jogging bottoms and a woollen sweater, I hailed a taxi and got in. As the hackney carriage trundled along the streets, the radio a dull lull in the background, I browsed through today's matches, scrutinising each one until I found the prized pig I was looking for.

3rd Place

MR DICKENS AND THE BAKEWELL PUDDING – A RE-IMAGINING

by Phyllida Scrivens

'So 'ow exactly did you create that tart young Anne? And speak the truth mind or there will be consequences'.

In the kitchen of The Rutland Arms, the finest hotel in Bakewell, Ann Wheeldon struggled to remember the ingredients and method, despite this being a dish she had prepared so many times before. But Mrs Wilson was a formidable woman and Ann wasn't feeling at all herself. If only her mistress Mrs Greaves would return from the Monday market, maybe she could then escape from this demeaning interrogation.

Less than two hours earlier Ann had opened the solid front door to welcome in Mrs Wilson, the wife of the town tallow-maker. She and Mrs Greaves often spent evenings together sharing local tittle-tattle and complaining about their husbands.

‘ ’ave I missed him?’ growled Mrs Wilson.

‘No, madam. He’s taking tea in the lounge.’

‘With your mistress?’

‘No madam, Mrs Greaves is downstairs preparing to go out on business.’

‘Pity. Then lead the way girl. You will introduce me to the great man.’

The whiskered gentleman was most gracious, inviting his visitor to take tea and ordering one of the establishment’s finest strawberry tarts. Ann was intrigued when Mrs Wilson seemed a little overcome.

In the kitchen Mrs Greaves was all of a fluster. The most celebrated author of the day was taking tea in her lounge and she had no choice but to deal with a double-crossing farmer, unashamedly threatening to raise the price of his Derbyshire Gritstone lamb. As she gathered up her heavy coat, Ann burst through the door.

‘You can’t go out now Mrs Greaves’, whined Ann, ‘the gentleman wants a strawberry tart and Cook is indisposed with the vapours again. Can’t Mister Greaves deal with the farmer?’

‘Don’t be impudent girl. You know he doesn’t get involved with our suppliers. You’ll manage, you’re well versed with the recipe. Now, has Mrs Wilson arrived?’

'Yes Mrs Greaves. She received your message and is sitting with the gentleman now.'

'Good. She will keep him amused until I get back. Now quickly girl. Get baking.'

And with that she swept from the kitchen.

In the lounge Mrs Wilson was in full flow. 'I confess I 'ave read all your works Mr Dickens. It is my ever so 'umble opinion that Dombey and Son has been the most edifying.' She paused, waiting for his response.

'Mr Dickens?

Charles Dickens was considering his belly. It was now at least twenty minutes since he had ordered that strawberry tart.

'Ah, yes, Dombey. My tragic triumph.'

'It is such an 'onour to meet you my dear Mr Dickens. With my 'usband and I being such 'umble people, I never dreamt it might be possible.'

Again, no response. Mrs Wilson tried again.

'May I 'umbly venture as to whether you are presently preparing a new great work Mr Dickens?

His eyes widened just a fraction. 'Indubitably, my dear Mrs Wilson. Young Copperfield. The manuscript is all but complete – merely a few minor character traits to enhance, maybe add the occasional irritating and habitual mannerism, annoying trait, create a unique voice....'

Despite her recent uncharacteristic fatigue, Ann's fingers deftly prepared the pastry, a skill she had learnt from her mother. It was second nature and she allowed her thoughts to relive a recent encounter only two months previously at Bakewell Monday Market. The young herdsman had been so gallant, taking her hand as she struggled to avoid a flooded pothole, whilst clutching her bag filled with eggs, carrots and parsnips, all the while aware of the water soaking the fabric of her long overskirt. Now, as she sifted and folded her flour, Ann struggled to remain focussed on the task in hand. She persevered.

'Now, I need to unroll this pastry around the pudding dish. Where has Cook put the strawberry jam?'

The young man with the green-blue eyes had invited her into the Castle Inn. There they shared a chocolate. Ann sighed and allowed herself to bathe in these memories whilst spreading a layer of thick jam onto the pastry case, before beating two hen's eggs until they were pale and frothing with air.

Why, she hadn't even asked his name or where he lived. Those moments shared together in the wood shed behind the inn had been magical. But, as God was her witness, she dearly wished she could tell him of the unfolding consequences.

Ann melted some butter on the stove, measured out sugar and ground almonds and added them to the egg mixture, stirring with a wooden spoon, all the while considering her predicament. As she poured the thick yellow froth over the jam her feelings moved to anger and self-pity. Heaving open the hot range door she placed the finished tart inside. Thirty minutes to wait.

Mr Dickens was becoming aggrieved at the delay and bored with the company. He could do with resuming his journey to Chatsworth. But not before he enjoyed the house speciality.

The moment Ann withdrew the dish from the oven she knew something was amiss. It looked nothing like her usual strawberry tarts, nor those of Cook, or Mrs Greaves. But it would have to do. She couldn't keep the guest waiting any longer. She pushed open the door of the lounge, sensing both impatience and obsequiousness.

'Finally,' snapped Mr Dickens. 'What kept you?'

Without waiting for an explanation he snatched up his silver dessertspoon and carved out a portion of tart. Mrs Wilson looked on, nonplussed.

'Wait Ann, what exactly 'ave you served to Mr Dickens? I 'ave not seen the like of it before.'

'Just a strawberry tart, madam. As the gentleman requested.'

Mr Dickens took his second mouthful. With flakes of pastry sticking to his moustache and dropping into his beard, he exclaimed, 'This is possibly the most sumptuous sweetmeat I have ever enjoyed. So nectarous, so delightfully pleasing to the senses.'

Mrs Wilson looked on as he devoured the remainder of this rather uninspiring sunken pudding, in her opinion resembling a poorly made Yorkshire. But seeing his enthusiasm, she became intrigued and began analysing the layers within the dish. It was certainly original.

Replete, Mr Dickens rose to take his leave, commending Ann for her cooking skills and sending his respects to the landlady. Dropping a silver shilling onto the table, he bowed to both women and left the building, a satisfied smile playing on his lips.

Ann went to follow him into the lobby but Mrs Wilson gripped her shoulder.

'Did you see 'ow much 'e enjoyed your pudding missy? Now, you and I will take a walk down to the kitchen, when you will tell me exactly 'ow you prepared it. I 'ave a notion that I may 'ave a proposition for you.'

As Mrs Greaves pushed open the kitchen door, she could just make out the hushed tones of a guarded conversation between her young employee and her neighbour Mrs Wilson. What were they up to? She knew Mrs Wilson to be an ambitious businesswoman who had been instrumental in building up her husband's candle-making business. She was scheming and falsely self-deprecating, constantly feigning humility to hide a ruthless streak. What did she want with Ann? But this intrigue would have to wait. Mrs Greaves had unfinished business.

'Come into the kitchen young Albert Hanbury. I intend to draw up my terms for next season's lamb order and you can deliver my proposal to your master. Such a shame he is indisposed.'

Ann looked up from her amateur sketches, an attempt to detail how she had prepared her pudding.

This was not proving easy for she had been much distracted. As the youth entered the room, cap in hand, Ann knew him instantly. Those eyes. Unmistakable. And now she knew his identity. This time he wouldn't get away. Standing and swiftly closing the kitchen door with a determined shove, she enquired, 'Will Master Hanbury be taking tea with us Mrs Greaves?'

TRIBUTE TO ANDREW HERON

1947-2018

As a tribute to Andrew, one of our most loyal, popular and talented members, lost to us in September, we would like to publish this tribute and Andrew's final story, entered into the Olga Sinclair Open Short Story Competition.

Andrew's love of poetry, fiction and biography led him to take up writing as a serious hobby once he had retired from his work in Further Education. He joined the Norwich Writers' Circle in 2007 and later successfully completed a number of creative writing courses, most notably with the Open University and at the University of East Anglia. Andrew particularly enjoyed writing short stories and poems.

With the Writers' Circle he found 'a home' for his writing, successfully entering many of the in-house competitions. In 2016 Andrew won three trophies, including the overall prize. He actively sought inspiration from visiting speakers, and enjoyed sharing ideas with his fellow writers. The Circle will miss him.

THE BEQUEST

by Andrew Heron

It was a raw February afternoon in 1849 when I visited my uncle in Newgate Prison, two days before he was due to be hanged.

The condemned cell was a narrow sombre room, separated from Newgate Street by a thick wall and receiving only a dim light from the inner courtyard. Seated on a long stone bench opposite the door was my Uncle Toby.

As my uncle rose slowly to greet me, I hardly recognised him. We had rather lost touch in recent years, but where was that brawny youth with a mane of flaxen hair, who had befriended me in my childhood and entertained me with dark tales full of wolves and dragons? Uncle Toby was now about 30 years old, some ten years my senior. Yet somehow he had become this stooping, pallid figure whose stringy hair had turned almost white. But at least those piercing blue eyes and sharp aquiline nose were unchanged. And when he spoke, his voice was as strong as ever.

'It's good to see you, Jack,' he said. 'I'm not

quite at my best, but I'm glad to have your company – particularly as I heard you'd been in a spot of trouble yourself.'

This was a reference to my ignominious flight from Cambridge six months earlier, after I had managed to burden myself with heavy gambling debts and the clinging affections of my philosophy tutor's wife.

'Yes, Uncle,' I replied. I've been lying low in Dublin for a while. It was only when I slipped back into London a few days ago that I heard you were here. But I'm afraid I know nothing of the circumstances.'

'Well, the bald facts are that I lost my temper and killed a man at "The Sly Dog" in Cripplegate. But there was a history between us that could work to your advantage, if you listen carefully and don't interrupt too often. First of all, though, what do you know of how I became the black sheep of our family?'

'Only that my father disapproved of your working in the street markets.'

Uncle Toby sighed. 'As his younger brother, I was expected to follow him into the legal profession. I joined the family firm as an articled clerk, but I just couldn't share his fascination with the subtleties of easements and codicils. Soon I found myself slipping out into the London streets. I was captivated by the sounds and smells of the sellers of fried fish, sheep's trotters, pickled whelks and penny pies; and all those street characters – the fire-eaters, sword-swallowers, spotted boys and pig-faced ladies, hurdy-gurdy men and sewer-hunters. Before long I fell for the charms of a costermonger's widow, and I abandoned the law forever.

'Within weeks, of course, the widow had in turn abandoned me, but by that time I'd chosen my new profession.'

'So what made you want to be a street patterer?' I asked.

My uncle winced. 'I'm not sure the term "patterer" or even "street story- seller" really does justice to what we do. Unlike costermongers, who merely peddle their wares, we're paid by people who want to hear us speak. No one bothers with surnames, but characters like Portsmouth George and Jemmy the Rake are known to one and all. And as I'll explain, there's no occupation quite like that of a death hunter.'

'A death hunter? That sounds sinister.'

'Not at all, Jack. Death hunters are true artists. We sell moving accounts of topical murders and the dying speeches and confessions of the culprits. The Bradford Tragedy, for instance – now there's a real winner. It draws tears to women's eyes to think that a beautiful clergyman's daughter could murder her own child; it touches every feeling heart. There's nothing like a stunning good murder. Take Rush, the Norfolk farmer – why I lived on him for at least a month. I worked my way to Norwich with Rush's "sorrowful lamentation," which I'd got up for the occasion. On the morning of the execution we beat all the regular newspapers hands down, for we had a true and unique account, and that beats anything they can publish. We had it printed several days earlier, and then stood with it right under the drop.'

'And does your work as a death hunter have something to do with why you're here?'

'I'm afraid it does, Jack. It's through death hunting that I met Ned the Cockmaster, the man I killed. Ned was an educated lad from a good family and, like me, he'd started in the law. He was training for the bar at Lincoln's Inn, but decided the roving life would be more exciting.

'We started working and drinking together, but we had rather different qualities. In good times, when there were plenty of murders, I'd do most of the work. I befriended gaolers all over the country, and persuaded them to let me visit prisoners. I became skilled at gaining the confidence of condemned men, who sensed they could trust me with their stories. Ned was lazier by temperament, but a real charmer with the ladies. So if there happened to be a female murderer, as in the Bristol Tragedy, he'd be sure to coax the best possible story from her.

'Ned also came into his own in leaner times, when we ran out of attractive murders. It's then that a death hunter with an imaginative turn of mind will resort to condemning some well-known person to death or serious injury. We call this a "cock" (as in a "cock and bull story") and Ned was certainly a master of the cock. He broke Prince Albert's leg, while the consort was out hunting, and he gave

Dickens a fatal and most affecting heart attack during a theatrical reading.'

'So if you and Ned were working well together, how did you come to fall out?'

'Well, despite all this, we began to have our differences – partly professional and partly personal. Where death hunting is concerned, I don't like too much fiction creeping in. When I've got a good reliable murderer like Rush with a lovely sentimental confession, I like to stick with him, knowing that I can comfortably work him another day. But then Ned started taking risks with our investments by spicing up the stories whenever he got bored or drunk. So in Rush's case, he managed to ruin our credibility throughout East Anglia by having Rush commit suicide in prison, and then appear as a ghost at Sir Robert Peel's family home. Of course, I didn't hold with this at all. When it comes to street literature, give me realism every time.

'But in the end,' continued Uncle Toby, 'it was something more personal that caused all the trouble. From the time we first met, Ned always had an eye for the ladies. They loved his strong athletic build, his shock of black curly hair and his swarthy complexion, which he put down to his mother's Romany ancestors. Most of his mistresses were in the Assize towns, where senior judges hear the most serious cases. Ned and I knew who the best "hanging" judges were, and would follow them on circuit, hoping for rich pickings.

But while I spent most of my time talking to the

condemned and their gaolers, Ned would be drinking ale and meeting local women.

'Anyway, none of this mattered too much to me until I met my Constance almost exactly 18 months ago in Winchester. Constance was so different from the girls Ned and I usually ended up with. She was a governess, an educated and virtuous woman with lively conversation, an elegant figure and teeth without parallel. We were married within six months of our first meeting, and Ned was our best man. All seemed well, although after a few weeks Constance began to look uncomfortable in Ned's presence and preferred not to be alone with him.

'I was delighted when Constance told me last April that she was expecting a child, but soon everything took a turn for the worse. She became listless and tearful, finding it hard to sleep during the long hot summer. Her confinement last November came several weeks early, and she lost a lot of blood during her labour. The surgeon told me to prepare for the worst, and at the end of a long night of suffering, Constance died. The child, a boy, was delivered alive, but never managed to breathe properly and slipped away in the late afternoon. But in the short time I cradled him in my arms, I could see well enough whose son that swarthy little boy really was.'

'So that's what brought you here, Uncle,' I said.

'Yes, it's not hard to see what happened next. As soon as I knew the boy had joined his mother, I rushed off to "The Sly Dog," where I knew Ned would be drinking. I got there just in time to overhear him rounding off a story of one his conquests: "So you see, there's more than one reason for calling me Ned the Cockmaster!" he guffawed, as he swept off his hat and bowed to acknowledge the raucous applause.

'Well, those were the last words he ever spoke. I rushed towards him with a bottle and brought it crashing down on the back of his head. He thudded to the floor, dashing his skull on a flagstone.'

'But was no compassion shown to you at the trial, Uncle?'

'No, it was a foregone conclusion, as I knew it would be. The case was heard at the Old Bailey, in front of Mr. Justice Spry, a fine old hanging judge who's been keeping death hunters like me in business for years. He offered no prospect of mercy, but then I didn't want any. I've nothing to live for, and the best I can hope for is to go out in style. I want to make a good death if I can, and preferably a memorable one. As luck would have it, I've known the gaoler here for years, having slipped him the odd commission for giving me access to prisoners. I've been introduced to the hangman, who's a jovial fellow despite having recently given up drinking. He's taken unusually careful measurements of my weight and height, and has promised to make sure the rope's exactly the right length for the drop. So I reckon it'll be quick, though maybe not quite as quick as it was for Ned.

'But I'm also thinking about what happens

after I've gone – and that's where I may be able to help you, Jack. For a while Ned and I were the best death hunters around, and we proved there's always a market for a lurid murder with a satisfying confession. Well, you're a sharp enough lad, Jack – even if you've led a rackety sort of life so far – and I know you like a good story. So how would you like to take over my business as a death hunter?'

'But I've no experience, Uncle,' I protested. 'I wouldn't know where to start.'

'If you speak to the gaoler, he'll give you an old oak chest with all my best stories, so you'll always have a good stock of reliable material. Not that I think you'll need it – there'll surely be hangings for as long as there are murderers and judges. And of course, just to start you off, I'll give you my own story, to do whatever you like with. Yes, it's an age-old tale of jealousy and revenge, but there's pathos too and quite a lot of irony. So it's all yours if you want it, Jack. Do you think you could make something of it?'

AUTHOR BIOGRAPHIES

Sue Ryder Richardson

It is an honour to win this year's Olga Sinclair competition. To write short stories is extremely rewarding, and it is a thrill to find that others enjoy your work. My local writing group encourages members to share their stories each month: the support they give is invaluable. I am also fortunate to attend regular instructive workshops with the Stradbroke Writers.

Louise Wilford

Yorkshirewoman Louise Wilford is a teacher and writer who has had work published in magazines such as Agenda, Acumen, South, Iota, Lyonnesse, Dreamcatcher and OWP, and has won or been shortlisted for several competitions. She is working on a fantasy novel and studying for an MA in Creative Writing.

Rhona Godfrey

Age 63; loves her Bus Pass. Works as a reader/scribe/ invigilator at Perth College. Her writing in 2018 has mainly been garrulous emails to friends, but she did win a 'Commended' award in June, in the Federation of Writers (Scotland) Vernal Equinox Competition, for her poem 'February'.

Iain Andrews

Although Glaswegian by birth and former citizen of Ipswich, Iain Andrews is now a proud resident of Norwich. He has had several articles published in trade and music magazines and has been shortlisted for two years running in both the Olga Sinclair and Wells Literary Festival Short Story Competition in addition to success in Writers Magazine competitions.

Kathy Joy

Kathy lives in Norwich with her husband, daughter, and Cavalier King Charles Spaniel. She is studying English Literature with Creative writing at the UEA. Previous published work includes the sci-fi horror *Last One to the Bridge.*

Peter Loftus

Peter Loftus is currently reading (and writing) for a Masters in Creative Writing with Open University. His short stories have appeared in Focus Magazine,

Visionary Tongue, Midnight Street, Albedo 1, Jupiter SF, and Monomyth, among others. He has been shortlisted for the Aeon Award and longlisted for the Fish Short Story Award.

April McIntyre

April McIntyre is a Cambridge-based writer and bedroom-based reader. She writes fiction and poetry as well as being a regular contributor of film reviews for HeyUGuys, ScreenWords and TakeOne. She also helps run the women's short film event, Reel Women at the Cambridge Arts Picturehouse as well as reviewing submissions and contributing words for the Cambridge Film Festival. She can often be found eating cake or petting cats on the street.

Mary Outram

A few years ago I did the Open University course: 'Start Writing Fiction'. It gave me the confidence to try and write more. I live in Yorkshire and enjoy the countryside. Some of my favourite authors are Tove Jansson, Bill Naughton and the poet Tomas Tranströmer.

Phillip Vine

Phillip has recently acquired an alter ego.
From 2019, his fiction will appear under the name P J Vine. His sports biography, Visionary: Michael

Knighton, Manchester United, and the Football Revolution will be published in 2019. He hopes a novel, The Last Song of Elvis Presley will follow shortly afterwards.

Phyllida Scrivens

Phyllida, currently Chairman of Norwich Writers' Circle, became a published biographer in 2016. An MA graduate in Creative Non-Fiction from the University of East Anglia in 2014, her first book Escaping Hitler was published by Pen and Sword. The follow-up, The Lady Lord Mayors of Norwich (Pen and Sword 2018) was awarded the Best Biography Prize at the East Anglian Book Awards in November 2018.

ABOUT THE NORWICH WRITERS' CIRCLE

In 1943, at the height of World War 2, a small group of enthusiastic creative writers, both amateur and professional, joined together and established Norwich Writers' Circle. The aim of the founders was to "encourage the art and craft of writing and promote good fellowship amongst Norwich and Norfolk writers generally.

The aim remains unchanged and it is in that spirit that our Circle continues to flourish today, with members work representative of a number of diverse literary styles and genres.

Over the years we have welcomed writers such as Louise de Bernieres, D.J. Taylor, Kathryn Hughes, Simon Scarrow, George Szirtes, Rachel Hore, Patrick Barkham, Alison Bruce, Hayley Long, Heidi Williamson, Keiron Pim, Elly Griffiths and Emma Healey.

We hold workshops and manuscript evenings when members offer constructive feedback to each other's work. Each season we offer opportunities for members and guests to enter in-house competitions, each judged by professional authors, with trophies awarded to our most successful writers.

And finally, we are proud of our annual Olga Sinclair Open Prose competition, with themes drawn from Norwich life, now in its fourth year, offering generous cash prizes to winning entrants. In addition members of the NWC have the opportunity for their entries adjudicated for the much-coveted Olga Sinclair Challenge Shield.

For more information please see our website at norwichwriters.wordpress.com

Or at facebook.com/Norwich Writers

Or email an enquiry to: norwichwriters@hotmail.co.uk

Printed in Poland
by Amazon Fulfillment
Poland Sp. z o.o., Wrocław